HAUNTING ON BEAR CROSS MOUNTAIN

A Vicki Ashton Paranormal Thriller

Book 1

By

Vicki Sutherland

DEDICATION

This book is dedicated to Mrs. Wilma Sueing, one of the greatest teachers and friends I know. She inspired my writing from an early age. Her influence, guidance, and friendship have meant so much to me through the years.

ACKNOWLEDGMENT

Writing a book is a journey that requires the support and encouragement of many individuals. I'm deeply grateful to those who contributed to the creation of this work.

I'm grateful to my family and friends for their unwavering support and patience and for sharing in my excitement of completing this project. They are my best cheerleaders.

I extend my thanks to the reviewers who meticulously reviewed the manuscript and provided constructive feedback. Your thorough assessments have played a pivotal role in enhancing the quality of this work.

I am grateful to Amazon Profs' David, Zoe, and John and their entire editorial and publishing teams for their support and enthusiasm throughout the publication process. Your commitment to excellence has made this collaboration a rewarding experience.

Lastly, I want to express my gratitude to my readers. Your interest in this book is both humbling and motivating. I hope that the ideas presented within these pages resonate with you and contribute to your understanding of *The Haunting on Bear Cross Mountain*.

Thank you all for being a part of this exciting journey.

Sincerely,

Vicki Sutherland

BOOK DESCRIPTION

Vicki Ashton and her friends are terrified out of their wits when they experience paranormal activity in an old, abandoned house next door and deep in the woods upon Bear Cross Mountain in Sparta, Tennessee. Strange events, such as drumming sounds, mysterious clouds of smoke, terrifying voices from disembodied souls, ghostly creatures, and poltergeist activity, lead them to research the history of the land. Will they find out what's causing these horrifying events and ghostly visitations? Will they be successful in ridding the land of its evil curses and restoring peace to their lives and their land?

CONTENTS

CHAPTER 1

It was back, with a vengeance this time. Gasped breathing, heart racing, feelings of dread and helplessness. The kind of sheer panic you can't control too easily because it grips you like the hand of death and won't let go. I felt it now, and every time I went near the garage. I didn't usually scare too easily, but the terror I experienced last week was difficult to overcome and impossible to forget. I was all alone, too, which made it even scarier, except for my German Shepherd, Keefer, who barked uncontrollably as though he saw something more than what I could see. My husband of 10 years, Terry Ashton, an aviation tech for Fed-Ex, was working in Knoxville that day until late.

I was stubborn enough to overcome the trauma, but I could never forget what happened. The memory was too vivid, and the trauma too deep. I saw it, though. I didn't imagine it, that mysterious cloud of thick black smoke fluttering above the garage. It was there. You couldn't miss it, just hanging there like some sort of alien cloud appearing out of nowhere. No rain. No fire. Just black smoke shimmering in mid-air, like a glider plane flickering in the sky, holding its own in a wispy wind. How could I forget something so bizarre?

Our garage was detached from the house, and I could see it from the living room window. That's how I'd seen the smoke in the first place, opening the blinds to capture a peaceful evening sunset. Welcoming nightfall across Bear Cross Mountain had become a tradition for me, a pleasant one, but this time, it was different. There wasn't anything pleasant about what I saw outside, and as my attention quickly switched from the dazzling sunset to the frenetic misty cloud above the garage, I started to panic.

Keefer wouldn't stop barking despite my "Down, Boy" commands. I wondered what it was that disturbed him so. I saw that smoke, but he seemed to see inside it or through it or maybe even beyond it. Was there more to that smoke than the eye could see? They say dogs have a much keener sixth sense than humans. Keefer must've been one of those. Whenever I took him for walks in the woods, his ears perked up, and he'd stare and growl like there was something more there than just the woods. It was downright spooky, and it was hard to calm him down.

I watched the smoke waft into twirly little tornados of vapor and encircle the whole garage like a smoggy haze shadowing the moon. At first, I thought the garage was on fire, so I raced outside helter-skelter like a madman escaping from an asylum. Ironically, there were no flames or smell of smoke anywhere in sight. Just a peculiar black mist that seeped right through the roof and walls into the garage.

Inside the garage, smoke was everywhere. It was so thick I couldn't see the ceiling above me or the walls beside me. Only the densely spreading smoke, spiraling upward like little smoke signals, forming ominous swaying figures in its mist.

Then, it coiled around me like a whirlwind as though I were the eye of its tornado. I heard voices in the circle, spine-chilling whispers, but I couldn't understand what it or they were saying. Werrrrrreeeeeeeeeer. Werrrrrreeeeeeeeeer. It reminded me of voices too low to distinguish above the sound of a buzzing fan. But they were there. I just couldn't make out the words.

My head was spinning as fast as the ghostly sphere around me, and it was hard to breathe. I was coughing, choking, suffocating, not from smoke inhalation but from my own heart-wrenching fear. I struggled to free myself from the spiraling circle, but it entangled me like a thickset web pinning me in its grisly catapult.

Somehow, I managed to break through it and snap a picture of the twiddling smoke with my cellphone. Maybe if I studied a picture more closely, I could figure out what it was. Suddenly, the smoke vanished from the garage just as quickly as it had appeared, evaporating like vapor rising from a steamy riverbed into nothingness.

I trailed it outside, hoping it was gone, but it was still there, glinting and swirling above the treetops. I watched in astonishment as it rippled through the roof and walls of the old, abandoned house next door. I snapped 4 more pictures and recorded 2 short videos. I needed to be sure I captured this once-in-a-lifetime paradox on camera. No one would believe it unless they saw it, so I needed proof.

I wanted to chase after the smoke but was too afraid to go inside the old house. After all, it was a creepy old house, dingy white with broken windows and worn shudders that creaked when the wind blew. The front door was tattered and barely hanging from its hinges.

Two big oak trees and a thick row of shrubbery along the side of the house partially blocked the view from my living room window. A rickety old wooden fence that looked like it would collapse any minute surrounded it and added to its shabby, run-down appearance.

Townsfolk said the old house was a popular hang-out on Halloween, the perfect hide-away for spooks and goblins and ghoulish pranks. I heard that a few trespassers through the years had tried to spend the night there but usually left scared out of their wits in the middle of the night with some spooky tales to tell. Don't know if they were true or not, though. It was just hearsay. Many declare it's haunted, but I didn't believe in such things. I couldn't explain the twirling smoke, though. Wispy vapor gliding through the air, appearing and disappearing at will? Harrowing voices in the mist? Maybe they were right.

A crooked and worn "No Trespassing" sign was stuck in the ground near the road in an obvious place for passersby to see it. Apparently, curiosity seekers trespassing had been a problem. I couldn't imagine why, though. I didn't understand why anybody wanted to go near it, much less inside it, to become the scapegoat of such lurid caliginosity. Some folks just craved a paranormal thrill, I guess, for whatever reason.

The old house belonged to a neighbor, Jim Hartwell, a retired widower, who lived by himself behind us about a mile away. The narrow gravel road beside us that curved around up a hill and past a pond was his driveway. We could see his rooftop from our backyard, but the house was mostly hidden from our view by hills and trees. His father, Earl Hartwell, used to live in the old house but passed away about

5 years ago. His ashes were buried back away on Jim's property and marked with a wooden cross.

Jim's mother, Sarah, and his late wife, Beverly, were both cremated and buried there as well. Sarah's grave was marked with a diamond-shaped headstone, and Beverly's was marked with a heart-shaped headstone.

Sarah passed away about 10 years ago from lung cancer, and Beverly died of COPD 2 years ago this August. But Earl's death remained somewhat of a mystery. Some say he died of old age; others say natural causes. Some even say there was something odd about his death that nobody can explain.

No one had lived in the old house since Earl Hartwell died. It just sat there, rotting away. I hoped Jim would have it torn down before somebody got seriously hurt there, but it sure seemed like he was taking his own sweet time for some odd reason. No one took care of the property except Jim, who mowed the grass every now and then.

Jim was 78 years old, of Cherokee descent, mentally spry, but physically moved quite slowly, with a limp due to an old army injury to his left hip. He usually wore blue jeans, a t-shirt, and a red flannel jacket since he was cold-natured.

I often saw him outside with his grandkids, riding his 4-wheeler through the wooded trails behind our houses.

Sometimes, he'd ride it up to his mailbox adjacent to my house on that 4-wheeler. He'd wave and smile as he passed by and was friendly and neighborly. He always had on that red flannel jacket, though, like it was glued to him. I never remember seeing him without it, no matter how warm or cold it was outside.

I'd regained my composure, was breathing normally again, and headed back inside my house when I heard a faint "tat-tat-tat" sound in the distance. It was the steady beat of a drum. Tat-tat-tat. It grew louder, then fainted, then loud again, which made it difficult to tell where it came from. I think it came from inside the old house, but I wasn't sure. It seemed to drift with the wind.

As the wind picked up, it was loud; when the wind died down, its beat was low, like it existed somewhere between the global world and an unknown firmament. But its steady beat tapped the same rhythm no matter how loud or soft the volume. Tat-tat-tat. Tat-tat-tat.

Eventually, the drumming stopped; the sound simply faded away like a windchime on a windless day. For a moment, the wind whistled its own eerie tune through the valley; then, lurid silence stifled Bear Cross Mountain with a gloom that made my hair stand on end.

There was a petrifying silence; I didn't know what to expect next and was afraid to find out. I could only anticipate it, like the calm before a brutal storm. It was coming, though... the storm... I felt it like a cold chill in my bones— a brutal paranormal storm, and I wasn't prepared for it or the gelid aftermath it would bring.

I glared out the window for several minutes, gazing back and forth from the garage to the old house. Keefer was still barking and jumping at the window as if he were trying to burst through it and attack whatever he saw. The paranormal activity had stopped, but its aftereffects lingered, and I felt shocked and numb from the inside out.

"Calm down, boy," I scolded and motioned him to sit beside me on the couch. He obeyed but growled angrily through his teeth.

My mind whirred with anxiety and fear of the unknown. Maybe the pictures I'd taken would tell me more. I scrolled through them and was stunned to find they weren't there. I'd taken 5 pictures, and the screen on each one was totally black. The videos I took played for their duration but were also totally black, and there was no sound.

How could that be? It was still daylight, and all the other pictures and videos on my phone turned out normal. Had something gone wrong with the camera setting? Did I accidentally push the wrong button and screw things up? I snapped a picture of the living room fireplace to test it. No, the camera was working fine.

This phenomenon happened a week ago, and I still panicked just thinking about it. I wasn't one to give up too easily on solving a mystery, but this one had me stumped. There was a logical explanation somewhere, I told myself, and I'd find it, but not today. I needed to block it from my mind and rest. I needed fun more than answers and a mental and physical break from the mayhem this had caused.

I hesitated but opened the garage door with the garage door opener. I had to face my fear sooner or later. This was the first time I'd stepped foot inside the garage since I saw the strange smoke; I couldn't leave my car parked here forever.

So far, the coast was clear, but I didn't want to be here any longer than necessary. I jumped into my Red Mustang Convertible and backed out into the driveway as quickly as I could. I peered inside the garage as the door closed to see if the odd mist had returned. Nothing. There was no smoke, no drumming, but I couldn't shake the feeling that I was being watched.

Ghoulish eyes stalked me from all angles. Shadowy beings vexed me with a translucent peril that made my skin crawl. Everywhere I looked, it was as though someone, or something, was staring back at me. Mystical activity was happening around me for sure, but I couldn't pinpoint where from or why. It was just a feeling, a creepy one, but nothing out of the ordinary happened.

You're losing it, Vicki Ashton, I told myself as I opened the convertible top, shifted my V8 engine into drive, and sped toward Hwy 111 south to Fall Creek Falls. Nestled in the Appalachian Mountains, it was my favorite state park and hiking spot. I planned to meet my best friend Robin Sanders there for the day to relax, grill burgers, and hike the Base of the Falls trail. I'd taken several trails there before, and it always seemed to soothe the soul, but today, it didn't turn out to be the relaxing getaway I'd hoped for.

The park was only about 20 miles from Bear Cross Mountain in Sparta, Tennessee, where we lived, but the scenic winding roads made the drive longer, about an hour or so. Captivated by its stunning beauty and laidback country ways, Terry and I moved here 3 months ago from Memphis.

I retired early, shortly after the COVID pandemic, from my 25-year job as an ER nurse at Memphis Methodist Hospital. I didn't miss it.

I loved being retired, but eventually, I wanted to do something part-time that I considered rewarding. I wasn't sure what at this time and didn't really care if it paid or not if it was a cause I believed in. Terry, growing weary of the corporate world and aviation's odd hours, planned to take an early retirement at 60 by the end of the year. We both looked forward to less work, spending more time together, traveling, and fixing up our new home.

The warm mountain air blew my hair every which way, but I didn't care. It was empowering, and I felt like I could conquer the world. I loved that carefree feeling, and nothing calmed my nerves like a beautiful country drive in the mountains. Besides, I'd gotten cabin fever from being cooped up inside the house for 4 days straight from all the rain we had lately.

Cooped up with my thoughts and fears about the recent hauntings, with no outlet from my own obtuse postulations. It was time to spread my summer wings and fly. I looked forward to a restful outing, and I certainly needed it. *But I had no idea the frightening news we would soon discover, nor could I predict the disturbing events that would occur when I returned home.*

CHAPTER 2

Robin was already grilling hotdogs when I arrived at our designated picnic table at the park. She wore blue shorts, a white tank top, and an apron that said, "Cookin' n grinnin'."

I laughed when I read it; the saying fit her to the tee like a fine-toothed comb. She was tall, nearly 6 feet, and thin, with straight brown hair that looped into a perfect angle under her chin, unveiling a natural Southern bell charm. She looked even taller, standing beside me with my 5'4" stature, and her hair looked almost black next to my shoulder-length light brown highlighted locks.

"Hey there, cookin' n grinnin'," I bantered, "I guess you're waitin' on these."

I handed her 2 hamburger patties and 2 pieces of sliced cheese.

The hickory-smoked aroma of the meat cooking made my stomach growl. Last week, I'd been so upset I couldn't eat much at all without feeling sick. Today, I was hungry enough to eat a whole cow, as some say.

"Well, it ain't a picnic without 'em," she said, placing the burgers on the grill. She joked a lot, was friendly and talkative, and seemed to never meet a stranger. I was just the opposite, a bit of an introvert and cautious about striking up conversations with people I didn't know.

However, the two of us shared an adventure streak that made us like 2 peas in a pod. We both turned 55 this year and planned to take a birthday Caribbean cruise together with our husbands in September.

I arranged 2 paper plates on a nearby picnic table, along with buns, mustard, ketchup, 2 Diet Cokes, and a bag of Cool Ranch Doritos.

Robin examined my table setting display with a frown. "No wine?" she criticized.

"If you want wine, you gotta come to my house," I said. "I ain't drinkin' and drivin'. I'll do one or the other, but not both at the same time."

Robin and I had lived across the street from each other in Memphis, where we grew up, and had known each other since we were 8 years old. We were in the same school, same grade, and same neighborhood until graduation, then we both moved to other areas of the city but always kept in touch.

Her husband, Coy, was a contractor and opened his own business, Sanders Construction, in Spencer, Tennessee, about 2 years ago. Terry helped him out some during his busy season, as he was also a pro at building, remodeling, and repairing things. Coy and Robin had introduced us to their realtor, who helped us find our house in Sparta. Fall Creek Falls was close by for us both and made a great meeting place whenever we decided to get together.

"I'll do that," she replied. "Come to your house, that is."

She finished grilling the meat, scooped it onto a platter with a spatula, then placed it on the table. "I could use a get-a-way. Coy is drivin' me plumb coo-coo. He's remodelin' the bathroom. Everything's outta' place. I can't find nothin'. Both he and the noise are givin' me the worst headache."

She and Coy had been married 20 years. When he wasn't building or remodeling for customers, he worked on projects at home, which Robin described as both a "blessin' and a cursin'."

"You ain't workin' this weekend?" I asked her. Robin was a professional massage therapist who worked from home, and Coy's many home improvement projects often interfered with her client scheduling.

"I can't work with all the racket he makes," she said. "My clients gotta have silence or soft music. Maybe if I stay with you for the weekend, he'll be done by the time I get back. On the bright side," she added, "the more he works, the less he drinks. I don't drink around him, so wine at your place would be great."

Coy had struggled with alcohol addiction for many years but had been sober for a year now. His AA sponsor, hard work, and Robin's stern reminders helped keep him that way, though I suspected it was mostly Robin's stern reminders more so than the other two.

"Sure," I said. "You might as well."

I grabbed a hot dog and hamburger and pasted 2 buns with mustard and ketchup.

"Yes, he'll probably be glad to get rid of me so he can work in peace." Robin opened the bag of Doritos, grabbed a handful, and then handed them to me. "And the feelin' is mutual."

"Sounds great," I said. "We can plan the excursions we want to do on our cruise in September. I can't wait to see Belize."

"Excursions?" she said, "That's easy. The guys will be with us, so food, drinks, sex, and the casino."

We both laughed. "Actually, no drinkin' for Coy, so that means more sex—and we'll find the nude beach."

She raised and lowered her eyebrows 5 times and grinned, which made me laugh even harder. I wouldn't be caught dead at a nude beach, but the thought was intriguing.

"But tonight," she said, "let's have wine and junk food night and watch a marathon of the ID channel and 24."

Our love for true crime shows and Jack Bauer were other things we had in common, and we watched them every time we got together.

"Great! Now, let's eat," I said. "Gotta keep our energy levels up for the hike."

"That's for sure," she said.

Since Terry was in San Diego on a business trip, it was the perfect time for a girl's weekend. Besides, with the strange happenings near my house, I was relieved that I didn't have to be alone. Maybe company was just what I needed to steer my mind from the paranormal happenings.

I hadn't told anyone yet, not even Robin or Terry, about the odd smoke and the mysterious drumming. I was afraid they wouldn't believe me. I wasn't exactly sure I believed it myself and putting it into words made it seem even more unbelievable.

Hopefully, it wouldn't happen again, I told myself, but my 6th sense screamed to every fiber of my being that this wasn't over. I ignored that inner voice and managed to shrug aside my concerns, at least for now.

But soon, the sixth sense would prevail and beckon me in ways I couldn't ignore.

CHAPTER 3

"Ready for that hike?" I asked Robin as we packed up our picnic supplies and locked them in our cars.

"Let's do this," she said, hiking sticks in her hands.

We loved hiking, especially waterfalls hikes, and had taken many trails in the Smokey Mountains and other parks throughout East Tennessee, Virginia, and the Carolinas. We had taken this trail numerous times and had never seen it this muddy. It was, however, passable, and the magnificent view made up for the extra trouble of getting our shoes so dirty.

Winding cliffs unveiled an enchanted paradise of bubbling waterfalls too magical to be real. It was mid-June, and recent storms had filled the frothy pool below the falls with more water than usual, making it ideal for a swim.

The tranquil swooshing of the falls echoed louder as we drew closer. It was truly a wonderland, and I couldn't wait to stick my feet in the water. However, Robin beat me to it.

"Damn, it's cold!" she shrieked. She waved a pair of muddy blue tennis shoes above her head in one hand and her hiking sticks in the other and was shivering all at the same time.

"I'm comin' in anyways." I waded into the rippling water and gazed upward at the roaring waterfall that sprayed cool mist onto my cheeks.

The stream was filled with children laughing, playing, and splashing while parents sat on huge boulders close by, watching them and chit-chatting among themselves. Some were walking their dogs. Some were picnicking. Others were sunbathing or meditating. Robin and I washed our shoes in the stream, then sat down on a big rock to rest and dry our feet.

"Have you painted any more pictures lately?" she asked.

"Yeah! Can't wait for you to see them," I replied. "I painted a landscape of the view of the pond and mountains behind my house to hang in my den, with the help of Valerie Dayton, that is. Do you know Valerie, who owns The Art Shop?"

"Yes, remember," said Robin. "I went to the art class with you and Connie LaForce. We painted a picture of the moon and the mountains; only mine didn't turn out so great. It looked more like a sad face behind a drooping planet Mars."

We both laughed.

I'd forgotten that Robin had attended an art class with me and Connie about 2 months ago. She quickly gave up painting, saying that it wasn't "her thing."

Since then, she'd taken up sewing and sculpting and was great at it. The blue curtains that she stitched and hung in her living room looked quite professional. She'd also sculpted an angel figurine of stone and several pieces of pottery from clay.

Art was my favorite hobby, and I often visited The Art Shop to paint. Connie LaForce was my main art buddy, and we often met there to further our skills in acrylics. Connie also owned The Hemp Market in Downtown Sparta on Spring Street and gave us discounts on smokes and edibles.

"I also painted a picture of a beach scene," I said. "I hung in the master bathroom, and I think I'm finally done decoratin', at least for now."

"Then, you're all moved in?" she asked.

"Yes, everything is perfect, well almost," I replied, "except for that old house next door. Jim really needs to tear it down; it's fallin' apart anyway. I call it 'The Nightmare on Rockman Street.'"

Robin started to reply but was interrupted by an unfamiliar voice behind us. "You ain't talkin' 'bout the Jim Hartwell house up there on Bear Cross Mountain, is ye, ma'am?"

I turned to face an older gentleman who sat behind us on the same rock. He was thin, in his late 60s, and wore blue jeans, black tennis shoes, an orange "Tennessee VOLs" t-shirt, and a matching cap. He spoke slowly with a distinct mountain drawl, pronouncing each word with two syllables whether they needed it or not.

"Actually, yes," I replied, "I live upon Bear Cross Mountain beside that old house. You heard of it?"

"Heard of it?" he said. "It's the spookiest old house in town. Everybody's talkin' about it. Won't nobody go up there unless they wanna see a haint?"

"A what." I chuckled—a bit surprised, though I knew "haint" was an old mountain term for "ghost." I'd heard it all my life, being raised in the south by a mom from Kentucky.

"A haint. You know—a spook. Folks have seen 'em up there too, spooks, that is." His voice ebbed deeper... slower... increasingly eerie.

22

"Ye do know its history, don't ye, ma'am?" He raised a bushy eyebrow and cast a daunting stare my way as though he were probing to find out what I knew rather than offering privy information about the old house. I was curious to find out what "history" he meant, so I played along.

"Just that Earl Hartwell died up there some time back," I said nervously. The old man was a bit odd, to say the least, and I felt uneasy around him, but I wanted to hear what he had to say.

Robin, who had been unusually quiet until now, exclaimed, "Somebody died up there. Eweeeee! You didn't tell me that!"

She was shivering again, more from craving an adventure than from being scared, I thought. She was naturally a curiosity-seeker, fearless, and loved solving mysteries. This one seemed to grip her, and I sensed her "detective ears" perking up.

The old man, stern and unsmiling, said, "It's *how* he died that's got folks a-talkin'."

He scratched his chin thinkingly. "Doctors told 'em one day he was fit as a fiddle, and the next day he dropped deader a doornail on the kitchen floor. A heart attack, some say. Others say he was scared to death by some sort of creature from the woods."

His voice switched from fast and loud to slow and deliberate, high pitched to low, and I felt even more leery of him. He reminded me of someone with multiple personalities, and I wasn't sure which one to expect, the calm one or the one that might lose control. "Jim found him lying there all wide-eyed and stiffened up like he'd seen a ghost or something," he added.

With a bleak smile, he extended his right hand to me and said, "By the way, ma'am, I'm Jessie Flatte. Lived here all my life right up on Chestnut Mountain Road." He shook my hand and then Robin's, and we both introduced ourselves to him.

I wasn't sure what to believe, especially since he seemed to be as confusing and mysterious as his story. However, I perceived he was leading up to something substantial that might shed some light on the haunting I'd experienced. "Tell us more," I said blatantly.

"Well," said Jessie, a bit surprised at my impudence, "when the medics got there, the house was full of smoke, but nothin' was burnin'. And they heard drummin', but nobody was playin' the drums. Weirdest thing ever."

24

His voice trailed lower, and he mumbled something under his breath, then raised his voice again. "Since then, folks in town have seen strange things up there. I've seen the smoke myself one evening up at Jim's while we was fishing—right at nightfall."

Jessie stood up and showed me his phone. "Somethin' else strange," he continued. "I took pictures, and this is what came out."

He scrolled through the photos on his phone and showed me 4 pictures that were totally black.

Now, he had my full attention. Smoke? Drumming? Blank pictures? So, I wasn't the only one who'd witnessed unusual activity next door. Jessie and Jim had also seen the smoke. What a relief to know. However, the reality of this whole ordeal petrified me to no end, and I yearned to find out all I could about this paranormal prodigy.

Jessie rattled on mostly about nothing, but my mind shifted to its own set of restless colloquies, so I barely heard what he said. Did the smoke and the drumming scare Earl Hartwell to death? An apparition? Some monster from the woods? A sinister being of some sort had caused these minacious events. Why was it here? What did it want? And what would it do next?

Jessie said a heart attack killed Earl Hartwell but indicated that something other than natural causes had triggered it. What did Earl Hartwell know about this supranormal activity that he couldn't tell us from the grave? What about Jim? He'd seen the smoke, but had he also seen or experienced other strange activities in the old house or on his property? I'd already decided to talk to him soon and find out.

It all seemed so farfetched, but fate had exposed me to a ghostly realm where the unknown and the unexplained materialized into loathsome realities and the abnormal acclimated to the mainstream. The questions in my mind wouldn't end; one answer led to 10 more questions, and they just kept coming.

Jessie handed Robin and I both a business card. I barely heard him say, "I install and fix heatin' and air units."

My mind was spinning like a top, trying to process all the new information and the questions I didn't know the answers to.

"Jessie's Heatin' & Air Service is right in town on Butler Street," he continued. "If yours ever needs fixin', just give me a call."

Still dazed, I stuck the business card in my shorts pocket. "Thanks, I will," I said, but my mind wasn't focused on heating and air units. It was focused on finding out whatever was haunting my garage and the old house next door.

"So... tell me more," I said anxiously to Jessie, "more about the old house and Mr. Hartwell."

"Well," he said, "rumor has it that old man Hartwell's place used to be a Native American reservation and burial ground back in the day. In fact, all that area up on Bear Cross Mountain was Cheer-kee land. After the Trail of Tears, white settlers moved in and built houses right over it."

He took off his hat and held it to his heart to show respect. "A cryin' shame, I'd say."

He shook his head in disgust.

"That smokey stuff they say it's Cheer-Kee smoke signals," he continued. "The tribe sent messages and warned each other that way. And they also sent messages of war to their enemies. To warn 'em they was comin' for 'em. And that drummin'? It's the heartbeat of the Cheer-Kee, their livin' dead. They live on. They live on, I tell ye."

Jessie wiped beads of sweat from his forehead with a handkerchief he stowed from his back jeans pocket. Then, he grabbed 3 bottles of water from a cooler that lay on the ground at his feet. "Water, ladies?" he asked, then handed one to Robin and me and opened one for himself.

"Thank you kindly," I said as I took the water.

The afternoon sun had gradually beamed into a large ball of sweltering heat—90 degrees at least. Drops of sweat ran down my back, and my underarms felt sticky. The cool water quenched my thirst like refreshing drops of liquid manna. I quickly felt rejuvenated, but when Jessie switched from calm mode to out-of-control mode and screeched to the top of his lungs like a slaughtered calf, all the energy gushed from my body like water from a broken dam.

"It's a warnin', I say! The Cheer-kee, they're comin' for ye." His wrinkled face switched from eerie to vicious, grotesque like a creature from a horror show, and I, the victim of his monstrous outburst.

"Ye moved on their land, and they don't want ye there." His body quivered with what appeared to be a painful and uncontrollable spasm.

He pointed his finger at me and shouted like a deranged lunatic, "If I was you, young lady, I'd get outta there as quick as ye can, cuz they're comin' for ye. They live on! Ye can't kill 'em, but they can kill you."

His shouts were boisterous, accusing, and spastic. Onlookers stopped what they were doing and gawked at him, then me, and their silence was as disturbing as their piercing stares. I felt humiliated, violated, and exposed by a spotlight of scouring atrocities and misconstrued disdain. If only I could run and hide, disappear like that smokey mist I'd seen, but there was nowhere to go.

Robin was tense, and I could sense her anger rising. *It was only a matter of time before she exploded,* I thought. I tried to find the right words to say to calm the awkward silence, but the words stuck in my throat like honey to its honeycomb, though not nearly as sweetly.

Robin wasn't feeling so sweet either, and she broke the silence with a fury I hadn't seen in her since the last time she caught Coy drunk. She squared her shoulders back and bellowed at Jessie in a voice as loud and disturbing as his, "Who the hell do you think you are you crazy old fuck! Leave us alone!"

She thrust herself toward him like a charging bull in a rodeo, then came to a deliberate screeching halt just inches from his disconcerted face. I grimaced, half expecting her to pummel him to the ground, but she didn't budge any closer, nor did she back down. Red-faced, pursed lips and her most vicious "fuck off" glare dared him to scream again. Stunned, shocked, he didn't move or utter a sound.

I was now more than ever keenly aware of the awkward silence around us. More stares. Anger, judgment. More curious onlookers standing, gaping to observe the outlandish commotion taking place among us. Robin resumed her seat on the rock beside me, put on her shoes, and grabbed her hiking sticks. It was time to go. The surging falls suddenly lost their tranquility and the mountains around us, their lusciousness. The babbling stream now trickled with tears of shock and gloom rather than refreshing droplets of Mother Nature's repose.

I felt the sting of the precarious stares behind us as we started up the trail back to the parking lot. Jessie squealed, "Don't say I didn't warn ye. They're there to kill ye, you'll never get outta there alive."

I cringed with anger and screamed, "Go to hell, you bastard."

"Mark my words, they're coming for ye," he yelled. "You'll see. You're as good as dead."

We kept walking and didn't look back, but the blistering echo of his heinous frenzy followed us and wasn't so easy to leave behind.

"That crazy old fart needs to be in the looney bin," said Robin.

At that moment, I decided to tell Robin about the smoke and the drumming, but Jessie's outrage sent her into such a ranting spell that I couldn't get a word-in edgewise. Besides, my voice quivered so much I couldn't talk. *I'd just have to tell her tonight when she came over,* I thought.

The trail back seemed long, and I left somber footprints behind me in the mud with each foreboding step. My body trembled like I'd been smitten by a cold, shivery wind. Robin tried to calm me with reassuring words but to no avail. I held back tears until I was alone in my car.

Then, the dam burst, and tears gushed from my eyes like a ravaging downpour. It seemed there was no escape from the fear, the smoke, the swaying apparitions, the drumming, or the perplexity of these disturbing incidents. I couldn't get Jessie's words out of my mind. "Ye can't kill em, but they can kill you. They're comin' for ye. Mark my words, you're as good as dead."

So much for a relaxing day! I arrived home feeling more terrified than ever. I parked my car in the garage with much more reluctance than ever before.

Fortunately, nothing strange happened, even though I expected the worst and still had that creepy feeling of being watched. Once inside the house, I sat down in the living room recliner and covered up with a warm blanket. Keefer hopped up in the recliner beside me, looking sheepish and calm. He knew I was upset, so he buried his nose in my blanket like a squirrel burying its head in a dark hole. That was his way of consoling me. I felt better already, knowing he was there beside me.

I'll be safe if I stay inside, I thought. But the loathsome echoes that followed me home brought no safety, no peace, no rest, and no relief in sight, and the paranormal storm had just begun.

CHAPTER 4

Smoke was everywhere, all around me. Thick, black smoke, so black I couldn't see the sky or the ground nor even my hands in front of my face. I groped the dark air around me and felt nothing. Nothing to see, nothing to hold on to, nowhere to go. I was in a deep, dark dungeon; it seemed, and sunlight a million light years away, a solitary confinement of smoke. Where was I? How did I get here inside this dark void of nothingness? The last thing I remember was coming home to find my house full of smoke. Everything after that was a total blur.

"Help!" I yelled. "Can anybody hear me?"

My plea fell on deaf ears. Nothing… but the soft, eerie whistling of the wind and the echo of my own desperate voice penetrating the grisly sphere.

"Help!" I yelled louder. Surely, somebody somewhere would hear me.

Hum-hum-hum, I heard in the distance.

"Is someone there?" I shouted.

Hum-hum-hum.

Ahead, a glimmering light shaped like a huge diamond appeared, and the humming grew louder. Had someone heard me?

"Over here!" I waved my arms wildly at the light, hoping they saw me and were coming to my rescue. But I soon discovered that the mysterious stranger was no rescuer at all.

The light glowed, then danced toward me. The closer it came, the hum turned into a buzz. *Buzzzzzzzzzzzz*, like a bolt of lightning vibrating through circuits of electricity in a maddening storm. The light transformed itself into a glowing figure, then separated into two forms, then a third, then a fourth. Each ghostly figure separated itself and formed another being.

First, there were 2, then 4, then 10, then I lost count. They were separating so fast that it was impossible to count them all. Hundreds of them everywhere, and slowly, they took form, Cherokee men and women in regalia and feathered headdresses.

I let out a terrifying scream that I thought would surely wake the dead. But the dead were alive and staring straight at me. Dark beady eyes, as cold as death. Then, I heard the drum. Tat-tat-tat. Tat-tat-tat. The heartbeat of the

Cherokee's living dead. *We live on. We live on.* Tat-tat-tat. Tat-tat-tat.

"The drumming will guide you. The drumming will guide you," the mystical figures swayed and chanted in unison. "The drumming will guide you to… to… to…"

"To what?" I asked them.

"The drumming will guide you to… to… to…"

"To what," I shouted at them.

I was screaming, "To what? To what?" When the phone rang.

I answered it on the 5th ring with a yawn and a groggy "Hello." It was Terry.

"Hello, honey bunny," he said. "Sounds like I woke you up."

"Yes, what a day," I muttered. I'd fallen asleep in the recliner after returning home from the park and, to my surprise, slept 2 hours.

"Much to tell you when you get back," I said, recalling the disturbing events with Jessie and the harrowing nightmare I'd just awakened from.

"Well, get your nap out," he said. "I won't be in the mood to sleep or talk when I get back and get ahold of you."

His tone was deep, jovial, and sexy.

"I won't give you a chance to sleep or talk," I teased.

He'd only been gone 2 days, but I missed him. His laugh. His touch. His jokes and even the silly songs he made up and sang to me. He radiated an energetic charisma that vibrated through an entire room when he entered, and I could always sense his presence without even looking up. His motivating force and get-up-and-go initiative kept me on my toes, though sometimes he could be overbearing and a bit bossy.

"You're still coming home Monday, right? "

"Yeppers," he said, "will be there around 4:00, and we'll eat at Marioochi's."

"Ciao Ryan and Coors!" I cheered. Marioochi's was our favorite pizza place in Sparta, and we ate there often. Beer, pizza, and bluegrass music were common traditions in the town square each week, and I looked forward to it every Monday evening.

My phone chimed and vibrated. It was a text from Robin. "On my way," it read, followed by a smiley face emoji.

I talked for a few more minutes to Terry, then said my "Goodbyes" and "I love you," and by the time I hung up the phone, Robin showed up at the front door. She barged her way into the kitchen carrying 3 big bags of drinks and snacks. Hershey's Kisses, Reese's Pieces, Cheese Dip, Hot Salsa, 2 bags of plain Tostitos, 3 bottles of Merlot, 3 bottles of Pinot Noir, and a 12-case of Diet Coke.

"Looks like you bought the store out."

I laughed and, in the same breath, said, "How much do you plan on eatin' and drinkin'? And how much weight you plan on gainin'?"

"Who gives a shit," she said.

"Let's get this party hoppin'. I don't drink around Coy, you know," she reminded me, "and it's been 2 months since I had a glass of wine."

She opened a bottle of Merlot and poured it into 2 oval-shaped wine glasses. We posed a toast to the best girls' night ever and placed our drinks and snacks between us on the living room sofa.

I turned on the TV. An episode of *The Scariest Night of My Life* was airing on the Travel Channel.

"Let's watch a few episodes of this." Robin downed her 2nd glass of wine and continued munching on chips and cheese dip.

"Some weird shit happens on this show." She poured herself another glass of wine and took a sip.

"Ain't sure I believe it all, but it's excitin' to watch."

A man on the show was sharing his story about paranormal activity in his attic. Voices, footsteps, crying, and moaning from disembodied souls haunted him during the wee hours of the night. He traced its haunted history back to a murder that took place there more than 100 years ago.

"Some of this stuff is pretty way out and unbelievable," said Robin. "It reminds me of that crazy old man at the park. That weird guy, Jessie Flatte."

I downed my 2nd glass of wine and was already feeling a good buzz.

"You mean *Dr. Jerkyll and Mr. Hyde*?" I laughed.

"Speaking of Jessie, I have a story of my own that I really need to tell you."

CHAPTER 5

It was storming now, and a tornado watch was in effect for another hour until 8:00 PM. Thunder crackled. Lightning flashed. Howling winds threatened the skies with deadly destruction amid Mother Nature's grueling wrath. I'd been afraid of storms since I was a teenager when a deadly storm badly damaged our house and left us with roof leaks and damaged siding to fix. At least now I had a basement in which to take cover if the winds got too rough.

The night waned, and so did the storm and the wine. Robin and I were on our 2nd bottle and quite tipsy when I told her about the paranormal events next door. She took the news with a grain of salt at first—along with drunken laughter and a lot more Merlot.

"You mean Jessie, that lunatic was telling the truth?" She let out a screechy cackle that was both ludicrous and so comical that I burst into my own frenzied chortle. I was glad I'd waited until we were both drunk to tell her. It was easier that way and not nearly as scary.

I opened the 2nd bag of Tostitos and Hot Salsa and kept munching.

"It happened," I said. "I saw it, I swear." I emptied the 2nd bottle of wine, opened the third one, then refilled both our glasses.

Robin held up her glass.

"Then, I'm going to pr-pr-pro-propose a toast," she slurred. "To the ghost next door."

Our glasses touched, and we both drank more wine. "To a long h-h-happy death—or life—or both—whatever the c-c-case may be."

We exploded into a utopia of laughter, and the chains of stress from the last week fell off my shoulders like shackles from a prisoner's ankles.

"Woo-hoo!" she roared. "Maybe the g-g-ghost wants a dr-dr-drink, too."

"Well, hell, let's drink one for him," I taunted. We did just that.

"A ghost can't drink anyway," I said. "He'd be like a skeleton walking into a bar and ordering a drink—and a mop."

Side-splitting howls of laughter followed, and, of course, more wine.

The storm raged on, and I was too blitzed to be afraid of its fury. Lightning flickered through the blinds like a neon sign blinking through a dark abyss. An unexpected crack of thunder blasted the skies so loud that I barely heard my phone chime. It was a text from my neighbor, Lori Ledford.

"You still awake?" it read.

"Yes," I replied.

"Do you have power? Mine's out."

Lori and her husband, David Ledford, were the first people we met upon moving to Sparta, and we became friends immediately. They were 50-ish, high school sweethearts, and had been married 30 years. They lived next door on the opposite side of us from the old house. She was Jim Hartwell's niece and half-Cherokee. They lived adjacent to Jim's house. A gravel road and pond separated their properties on 50 acres of wooded land around them.

I dialed her phone number.

"Come on over," I said when she answered the phone.

I put the phone on speaker and said, "Say hello to Robin."

Robin and Lori exchanged hellos. They were also good friends, and the 3 of us went to plays and movies and out to lunch together quite often.

"Not sure what's goin' on," she said. "Power has been out for over an hour."

She sounded worried. "David and Jim left today for a 2-day fishin' trip at Whiteoak Lake in Oak Ridge. They're stayin' in a houseboat there and won't be back 'til Sunday, and hopefully with a trunk full of trout."

"Wow," said Robin, "If it's rainin' there like it is here, that houseboat is a-rockin'. Hope they're okay."

"They just texted me and said everything is fine," said Lori. "They still have power, but I don't."

"Well, come on over," I said. "Terry is in San Diego until Monday. It's just me and Robin here. I'm sure the 3 of us can find some trouble to get into."

"On my way," she said. "Thanks."

The storms had died down, and it was nearly 8:30 when Lori arrived. She wore Hello Kitty pajama bottoms and a black top and changed into her house slippers as soon as she entered the front door. She had short black hair, which stunningly revealed her Cherokee heritage, was extremely thin, and the pajamas swallowed her whole.

"I'm ready for the slumber party." She giggled. I poured her a glass of wine, and we proposed a toast to her and the best pajamas in the world. Soon, she was as woozy as we were.

Robin was singing to the top of her lungs, "Yesterday, all my troubles seemed so far away..."

An avid Beatles fan, I sang along with her, then transitioned to *"We All Live in a Yellow Submarine."* Lori joined in singing with us as we each found a comfortable seat on the living room sofas.

An episode of *Evil Lives Here* was showing. I turned up the volume, and the 3 of us quickly became glued to the screen. A lady who had unknowingly married a serial killer was telling her incommodious story of her husband's aberrant behavior and how he'd raped and murdered 5 victims, unbeknownst to her, before being arrested.

During the commercial, I asked Lori if she'd ever seen anything strange next door at the old house. She was quite knowledgeable of the ancient tribal traditions of the Cherokee, so I thought she might know something about the weird hauntings or the history of the ancient reservation and burial ground that once existed on the land.

I was right; she did know more, but I wasn't prepared for her response. Her ambiance quickly switched from upbeat and exuberant to one of despair with a grave silence, and at first, I regretted asking the question. She turned off the TV and stared at me stony-faced, tearful.

"I-I-I thought it was just me," she said timidly.

"You're not the only one," I reassured her.

She choked back tears. "The shaman—the medicine man," she said, "used to practice healin' and voodoo at his quarters, which was where the old house next door to you now stands. When he healed someone or cast a spell, he would always call for smoke signals and drummin'."

She buried her face in her hands to hide more tears.

"I believe you," I said. "I've seen that smoke and heard that drummin'."

"You have?" she asked, surprised yet relieved.

"They came to me in a dream," she said, trying to hold back more sobs. "It was so scary, and it seemed so real."

She wiped her eyes with a paper towel and took a long, deep breath.

44

"I saw a light shimmerin' toward me," she said, "and it kept separatin' and formin' more and more figures—they were all Cherokee men and women. They were chantin' and drummin'. And-and-and…"

She took a sip of wine, hesitated, then took another sip.

"And they said the drummin' would guide me to somethin'. I kept askin' "to what," but I woke up before they could tell me what it would guide me to."

CHAPTER 6

How could Lori and I both have the same dream? It was not only freaky but one in a million chances, if that much. Coincidence? Not likely. Did the Cherokee cast some sort of spell over the land years ago that oppressed its habitants with ancestral nightmares?

Were we both on some numinous wavelength with these spirits, enabling them to unveil the same messages to us clairvoyantly? What were they trying to tell us? What was the mysterious drumming supposed to guide us to? Was there something hidden on the land or in the old house that they wanted us to find? If so, what was it, and why and how could we find out?

It was Saturday morning. I woke up at 8:30 AM with these questions vexing me, and I couldn't go back to sleep. I was exhausted. Every muscle in my body ached, and I had a severe migraine that wouldn't tolerate light, noise, or nonsense. Wishing there was a morning-after pill for hangovers, I stumbled into the kitchen and decided that brewing a pot of coffee would be the next best thing.

Robin was sound asleep on the living room sofa and snoring loud enough to wake the whole town. I assumed that was why Lori had gone to sleep in the guest bedroom and closed the door.

I poured myself a cup of coffee and sat down in a patio chair outside on the front porch. This was my favorite morning meditation spot, especially during the summer. I watched the cows and horses graze on the rolling hills of the farm across the street. Bright red barn, rich green grass, and crape myrtles blooming pink and white cast different color sparkles on the rippling pond. The sun peeked through puffy clouds and showed positive signs of a clear day. Yesterday, the 3 of us talked about hiking a trail behind David and Lori's house that led to a waterfall. The weather looked promising for such an event, and I wanted to go. I never got tired of waterfall hikes; I'd done 2 the past week and was ready for more, usually averaging about 5 a month.

I finished my coffee and returned to the kitchen. Robin and Lori were awake but grunting and groaning from what I called *The Hangover Blues*. Lori poured Raisin Bran into 3 bowls while Robin made toast and more coffee. I placed butter and blueberry jam on the countertop. We ate in silence and consumed enough coffee to float a boat, it seemed.

Now, I felt miserably stuffed, and my head was still pounding. I took a CBD gummy I'd bought from Connie at The Hemp Shop, drank a cup of water, and then went back to bed. In anguish, I lay there still as a mouse under a soft, warm blanket. Soon, my mind was calmer, and I fell into a deep, blissful sleep.

I woke up around noon, feeling rested and relaxed. My headache was gone, but I was thirsty enough to drink a river dry. I poured myself a glass of water and drank the whole thing in one big gulp, then refilled my glass and drank more. Water only for me today, I scolded, and lots of it.

Robin and Lori were both dressed in tee shirts, hiking shorts, and tennis shoes, spry and ready to go.

"It's about time you woke up," said Robin. "Times-a-wastin'. Let's go hikin'."

She fastened a black backpack over her shoulders.

"I'll wait for yawl outside," she said as she exited the front door.

"We packed a picnic lunch," said Lori. "You'll love this place. It's about 2 miles behind our house."

She grabbed a blue backpack and then left to join Robin outside.

I was dressed and joined them outside on the trail within 10 minutes. Everything looked perfectly normal as I passed by the garage and the old house. I kept glancing back to see if the smoke or anything direful appeared. Nothing. All was peaceful, at least for now, *but that would soon change.*

We made our way up the gravel road, passed the pond and Jim's house, and passed the Hartwell gravesites, then soon found ourselves in a luscious field of trees and flowers and blooms of every color in the rainbow.

Several large trees had been uprooted, I assumed, by the storm, creating a perfect spot to sit and watch the wildlife. I snapped a picture of 2 squirrels as they chased each other up a tree. A deer dashed through the woods as if to play hide-and-seek from probable hunters. A group of wild turkeys, at least 6 that I could see, peeked through the bushes, and gobbled among themselves. Robin and Lori snapped pictures on their cellphones, too. I hoped they'd capture pictures of things I may have missed.

We pushed on through the thicket and came to another field. The grass was much taller here, about knee height, and resembled blades of gold and purple wheat swaying gracefully in the warm summer breeze. We came to a bluff, a tall embankment of rock, moss, flowers, and grass, and there it was, the majestic waterfall streaming down the mountain into a rocky stream about 100 feet below us.

Enthralled by its beauty, I snapped pictures of the waterfall, the stream, the woods, and a few red birds on nearby trees. We all agreed that it was the perfect spot for lunch, peaceful and luscious. Lori spread a blanket on the ground, and both she and Robin placed their backpacks on top of it. They had come prepared with all the items we needed for the perfect picnic. Paper plates, napkins, pimento cheese sandwiches, chocolate chip cookies, BBQ potato chips, and bottled water.

We ate lunch while the crickets chirped. Bullfrogs croaked. Streams trickled. Winds whistled. Birds tweedled. It was a perfect harmony of song... *Nature's Choir*. But deep within the woods, there was a sound I hadn't heard before. It whistled, but it wasn't the wind. It hummed, but it wasn't a bird. Its timbre was shrill but smooth and steady. Sad but lustrous, each note lingered then faded gently into the next one in a smooth but lamenting requiem. It was both beautiful and unsettling at the same time... and it beckoned me.

"Do y'all hear that?" I nudged both ladies, and they strained to listen more closely.

"Hoooo-oooh-oooh-oooh-oooh-waaa.

"Hoooo-oooh-oooh-oooh-oooh-waaa."

"A flute," said Lori. "A Native American flute."

"Hoooo-oooh-oooh-oooh-oooh-waaa.

"Hoooo-oooh-oooh-oooh-oooh-waaa."

"Let's follow the sound and find out who's playin' it," said Robin. Her adventure streak had kicked in full force, and I knew by the excitement in her voice that she was going, with or without us. Lori and I both agreed to go with her if only she'd go first.

We left our stuff and headed into the woods, empty-handed except for our phones. Robin led the way, ears perked and footsteps hot on the heels of the somber flute tones. Hoooo-oooh-oooh-oooh-oooh-waaa. Lori and I followed a bit sheepishly at first. Then, as we became closer, my curiosity overturned the fear of danger I'd felt.

We scrounged our way through a thick patch of shrubs, vines, and briars. The flute tones sounded louder. Closer. We were almost there. Directly on the other side of the bushes where I'd crouched down to crawl through, there it was. Unmistakably loud and clear.

Then, like a deer in heat, I barreled through the thicket, skittish yet determined to catch a glimpse of the mysterious flute player. No one was there. No flute player, and the flute tones faded again, barely audible above the sound of the trickling stream.

"That's weird," I said to my friends. "It was right there."

I pointed to the briary underbrush beneath me. "The flute player couldn't have gotten away that fast."

"Let's keep tryin'," said Robin. "Got to be around here somewhere."

This time, the ominous flute tones led us through the woods, up a path, and around a hill. Hoooo-oooh-oooh-oooh-oooh-waaa. Then, into the most baneful part of the forest, it seemed. The tree branches resembled huge black arms with claw-like tentacles pinching at us, trying to draw us into their rancorous pit. Hoooo-oooh-oooh-oooh-oooh-waaa. The tones grew louder and a bit more melancholic. The air was dark and chilly, like a dismal tomb buried deep in a shadowy pit of the maleficent unknown. Hoooo-oooh-oooh-oooh-oooh-waaa. It was calling…

Louder. Closer, so close I could reach out and touch the flute player, I thought. I tore through the thick

52

underwood like it wasn't even there and... nothing. Nobody and the flute tones faded and ebbed into the silent realm from which they came.

"What the hell?" I said, more to my bewildered self than anyone else.

"How could that be?" asked Lori.

We were out of the woods now and back in the sunny field by the waterfall where we'd left our picnic supplies. Our mystery flute player had led us in one big circle and left us baffled, to say the least. Where did the sound come from? Why couldn't we find it? Who was playing the flute?

"Well, that led us nowhere," said Robin, disappointed that we hadn't solved the mystery. "Now, what?"

As puzzled as we were, I wasn't going to let it ruin my day.

"The day is young," I assured her, "and there's still time for a selfie. Now take your places, ladies."

We gathered in front of the waterfall, and I snapped a selfie of the 3 of us. They took pictures with their phones as well. Then, we packed our supplies and headed back toward my house. I snapped more pictures along the way.

One of a ground hog peeping from behind a tree and another of 2 rabbits chasing each other in a field of butter cups. I wondered how this place could be so enchanting yet portentous. Invigorating yet grim. Charming yet bewitching. Beautiful yet baleful, all at the same time.

Bear Cross Mountain was known for its beauty, and it didn't disappoint, but discovering its malevolent past and vitriolic spirit activity did. I wondered what it was like in the beginning when the Cherokee lived here. Was the land ever at peace? If so, what changed that? Why did they still haunt the land? Did they have some unfinished business to take care of here before their spirits could rest in peace? So many questions with so few answers.

It was approaching 4:00 PM now. A few thick clouds shaped like big snowballs had tamped the sky along with a billowy stream of white smoke tailing a jet plane flying by. It wasn't until Robin and I had sat down on a big rock to rest that I noticed Lori had stayed behind quite some distance.

"Is everything okay?" I asked her.

But I knew something wasn't okay. She stood still as a statute and fixated on something, but I couldn't see what. Something in the woods? Maybe a bobcat, a snake, or a coyote?

Before I could ask, she let out a bloodcurdling scream and scampered like a scared rabbit onto the rock between us. Quivering, crying, I thought my arm would fall off, and she gripped it so tightly.

"What's wrong?" Robin and I both asked.

Alarmed and shaken, we both placed a hand on her shoulder to try and calm her. "It's okay," we both assured her.

"The smoke." Lori pointed at the woods like it were a foreign object, emitting toxic miasma into the air around us.

"I saw smoke in the woods. It followed us, then it disappeared about 10 feet away from me."

She was wheezing and gasping in such a frenzy that, for a moment, I thought she'd faint.

"First the flute, then the smoke," she said. "The medicine man is here. He will heal some and kill some. He will bless some and curse others. *The tribe always played the flute to welcome his arrival. He's here.*"

Medicine man? I didn't see him anywhere. In fact, I didn't see anything and thought Lori was just being paranoid. I suggested we head home and make some sweet tea and soak up some sun rays. We did so, but it was a silent journey.

Tense and the restless emanations among us were evident and so thick you could cut it with a knife. We were freaked-out and edgy. It seemed like a black cloud followed us home and wafted over our souls like the grim reaper beckoning his chosen dead.

The effects of the gummy I took earlier had worn off, and I was ill-at-ease and jittery. I glanced over my shoulder, constantly expecting something scary to happen. I snapped at both ladies and jumped at every little sound. A bundle of nerves, I couldn't calm down no matter how hard I tried.

I thought of drinking myself into a stupor like last night; then, I remembered how terrible I'd felt this morning. I was at a loss for what to do about these hauntings or if anything could be done. I was tired of not knowing what to expect next and being afraid to guess.

Exhausted and drained, I could sleep for a month, I thought, *but my mind wouldn't let me.* It was like my brain had a rechargeable battery inside it, constantly charging itself and never wearing down.

We all kept our silence for about a half-hour at least. Then, we spoke but avoided the obvious issue—the mystery flute player and the medicine man. Nobody knew what to say, but we each knew what the other was thinking.

If the medicine man was here, then why couldn't we see him? What was supposed to happen while he was here? Why were all these ghostly events happening to us? Who could we tell? Who could we trust? Who would believe us? How could we make these frightening things go away? Still, no answers.

"Anybody up for a game of Gin Rummy?" I asked. I was trying hard to focus on something different and give my mind a rest.

"We may as well," said Robin.

"I'm in," said Lori.

I went inside and came back out with a deck of cards, a pad of paper, and a pen. Keefer followed me outside and was restless, so I thought it best for him to get some exercise. He romped around in the yard and then ran off into the woods with Lori's pet collie, Hunter. They often played together like 2 best friends. I knew he'd be back when he was through exploring.

We played cards outside until it got dark, and then, we moved inside to the dining room table. I glanced up at the clock to find it was 8:15 PM. The time had flown by, and even though I was winning, I was ready for a break.

In the kitchen, I realized it had been more than 3 hours since I'd checked my cell phone. There was a missed call and a text message from Terry that said, "2 more days." And sent 5 heart emojis.

I texted back, "Can't wait." And added 5 heart emojis. Then, I remembered in all the drama of the day, I hadn't even looked at the pictures I'd taken earlier today on the trail.

I sat down in a chair and scrolled through them one by one. There were at least 50 pictures. Photos of the wildlife, woods, trees, flowers, and mountains. I was known for getting "snap happy" on vacations or hikes and at events. I took at least 10 pictures of the waterfall.

Yet, there was one that specifically caught my eye. Something very strange about this one. The selfie I took of the 3 of us in front of the waterfall showed 4 people in the picture. I enlarged it to get a closer look. There was Robin, Lori, and me, then an image that was faint and shimmery. I could see right through it, but it had a form. *The form of a Native American man playing the flute.*

CHAPTER 7

Had the mystery flute player been with us the whole time in the woods? Had he followed us home? Was he with us now? Was he spying on us? Maybe he was just a prankster who led us on a wild goose chase just to waste our time? Who knew? I was hesitant to show the picture to Robin and Lori for fear that it would cause further distress, so I decided to wait until a better time.

But I was glued to the picture, enlarged it, and stared at it multiple times before closing my phone. Absolutely no doubt. I'd captured the apparition of our mystery flute player on camera.

It was the last night of our girl party, and we were so stressed that I suggested we do Yoga. The ladies agreed. I taught yoga for 2 years at Cross-Fit Fitness in Memphis and considered it one of the best stress relievers for mind and body fitness. We each grabbed a yoga mat from the living room closet, as well as a block for positioning and a strap for stretching. I streamed a Yoga lesson from Amazon Prime, and we spent the next hour bending and stretching and deep breathing.

We practiced awareness and being in the moment from the first mountain pose to the end of the video; I guided us through a few extra hip and low back stretches and extended the final relaxation time for an extra 10 minutes. I dozed off for a few of those minutes, and it felt great. My body and mind felt lighter, and I could think more clearly. Robin and Lori were calmer, too, and we talked about getting together for a Yoga session weekly.

After a while, we decided to watch a few episodes of the show 24, Season One. I'd seen it multiple times, but I always enjoyed watching it with someone who hadn't seen it before. It was Lori's first time, so I was super-excited. We sat down on the living room sofas. Finally, I thought we'd finally have a pleasant night of fun without anything out of the ordinary happening. *But I was dead wrong.*

We watched 3 episodes of 24 and decided it was time for a break, so we decided to go outside and roast some marshmallows. It was nearly midnight and such a cool, pleasant night. I had plenty of wood for the firepit, so we sat down in lawn chairs on the deck beside it. I lit the fire, and soon, the smoke sizzled through the firepit chimney like a hot wind rising from a desert dust storm.

We also used wire hangers to roast our marshmallows, like 3 kids at camp. Two was all I could eat, but I loved roasting them. Most of the time, I was too impatient and let them catch on fire and would eat them charred. They were still good that way. The fire started to dwindle, so I threw another log on it to keep it burning.

Crackle. Crackle. Crack. It felt warm and soothing to my legs.

It appeared to be the ideal night. A full moon formed a perfect white circle above us and made it easier to spot the big dipper and a few other constellations. I could see my friends and my whole back yard in the twilight, and the fire made it even brighter. It was seldom ever this bright at night; I could've walked through the woods and found my way by the light of the moon if I'd wanted to. Apparently, Keefer felt the same way. He'd returned from the woods and was lying down on the deck as well.

"What a beautiful night," said Lori, reclining in the lawn chair as if she were preparing for a nap.

"I wish I could freeze this moment," she added.

"Me, too," said Robin. "Freeze the moment?"

A freeze was coming, but it wouldn't be this moment that brought the icy-cold chill that pierced me to the bone and made my hair stand on end.

The stars and planets all aligned together and lit up the crepuscular sky with one spectacular light show that seemed to brighten the whole universe. A magical display of stellar ensembles across the heavens. I wasn't the only one watching it, though; not by far. Lori and Robin were captivated… and… *there were others*. Others that brought that pins-and-needles-type cold where you couldn't feel anything, not even your fingers and toes.

"What was that?" Robin shrieked like a siren going off to warn bystanders of a deadly storm ahead.

She'd felt that same sudden burst of cold air that I felt. It startled me, so I jumped to my feet and spun around to see where this Arctic blast came from. I didn't see anybody, but a huge shadow covered the whole backyard with a shroud of blackness and a stifling sense of… death.

I rubbed my hands together to try and create some warmth in my fingers, but a growl as deafening and horrid as the darkness itself penetrated the ghastly zephyr, and my whole body felt like an ageless statue frozen in sub-zero time. My teeth chattered; my knees were knocking. We were all shivering, gasping, trying not to scream. What was there?

Something... others... from the dark abyss of the amorphous underworld invading our stillness by the light of the moon. We felt it. We heard it but couldn't see it.

It growled and made raspy breathing sounds like a killer beast on the prowl, but it was unlike any beast I'd ever heard before. Undoubtedly, it was inhuman, other-worldly. It had no form that I could see, just a huge mass of shadowy blackness twisting in circles and forming a blustery vortex of pure evil and sheer terror. It touched me with its frosty breath and threatened me with its barbarous gnarls.

Right in my ear. Growling. Breathing. Grasping at the nape of my neck with what felt like spiky claws or jagged-sharp teeth ready to devour me. The vortex twirled at high speed and felt like a huge fan out of nowhere gusting down on me from an invisible firmament of indescribable hell. My whole body was numb. I didn't move a muscle. I was afraid it would grab me if I did, so inside, I raged in terror but stood perfectly still on the outside with a deafening silence.

I was inside the vortex now and felt it zap me from the ground like a giant vacuum sucking me into its distorted whirlwind. I fought back, kicking and trying to wiggle myself free, but was powerless against it extracting force. I was twisting and twirling in all directions: right to left, then around and around. The rumbling whir of the vortex wind was so loud it drowned out everything else. I couldn't even hear my own voice crying out to Lori and Robin in desperation.

"Lori, Robin, where are y'all?"

No answer.

Apparently, I was too far away and drifting farther into this whirling tunnel of darkness that had no beginning or end and no light. Where was this thing taking me? A dark realm of torment and agony? An unknown world of cruelty and evil? What did it want from me? All I knew was that I had no control over where I was, what I heard or saw, or where I was going. I couldn't see Lori or Robin or my backyard or anything anchoring me to my reality.

Just… breathing… growling… whirring… twisting… twirling…

Finally, I thought I heard Lori's voice, but it was so faint. "Tsul 'Kalu, be gone." Maybe it was a dream…

"Tsul 'Kalu, be gone." I was drifting in and out of… "Tsul 'Kalu, be gone. Leave now."

It was Lori. Her voice was much louder now, and her confidence was unshaken.

When I opened my eyes, I was lying in the middle of my backyard, feeling like I'd been assaulted, stabbed, wounded, and left to die.

"Are you okay?" Robin asked.

"I'm not sure," I said.

Lori was learning over me, still saying, "Tsul 'Kaul be gone."

And whatever that thing was, it left with a buzzzzzzz. It sounded like an electrical current short-circuiting from my yard to next door, where it exploded like a torpedo in a combat zone, leaving behind a thick cloud of black smoke that covered the whole yard.

The eruption disturbed a flock of ravens; at least 50 of them squawked and scattered in all directions to escape its fiendish blaze. The shadow it had cast in the yard slowly disintegrated, turned into smoke, and drifted above the yard, to the garage, and then to the old house, like before.

Keefer and Hunter were spastic; growling, howling, and barking at whatever that thing was, the birds, the smoke... and I heard other neighborhood dogs growling frantically as well… owls hooting… night creatures fluttering through the trees trying to escape the unrest that thing, Tsul 'Kaul, had left behind.

Then came… tat-tat-tat. The drumming was coming from inside the old house for sure this time. Tat-tat-tat, tat-tat-tat. The shaman, the medicine man, was here. What would he do? Had he come to do good or to do harm or some of both? Would he heal, or would he kill? Was anyone with him?

Yes, there were others. Others… that followed. And others… that never really left but only hid until an appointed time. Did they ever leave? I doubt it; they only remained silent until something stirred their sentiments or brought to life their grieving souls.

When I calmed down enough to speak, I asked Lori, "What the hell is Tsul 'Kalu?"

She had proven that her Cherokee blood ran deep and that she was aware of what we were up against. Somehow, she'd known innately what to do and commanded Tsul 'Kalu, whatever that was, to go away and save me from unimaginable horror. She'd pulled me back into this reality with her quick thinking and Cherokee knowledge.

Tsul 'Kalu could be invisible or visible. It was known as the slant-eyed or sloping giant in Cherokee legendary folklore. Visibly, it was a monstrous beast about 9 feet tall, and some called it the "Cherokee Devil" or the "Cherokee Sasquatch" because it had similar features to that of Bigfoot. Gorilla-like, ferocious growling, raspy breathing that made your skin crawl. Some had seen it in person, been chased by it, and lived to talk about it.

Those incidents usually happened deep in an uninhabited forest where only the brave dared to go. Some also entered the woods and were never seen or heard from again. Still others had been slaughtered by its bloodthirsty raids, and their remains were found in shreds, too mangled to identify them. Others, like me, had been tormented by its invisible form.

Tsul 'Kalu possessed the ability to read and control minds, to disappear and reappear quickly or remain invisible, making it easier to surround and victimize the vulnerable. Greatly feared by the Cherokee, legends report that its footprints can still be seen on the banks of North Carolina's Tuckasegee River.

A museum there, according to Google and Lori, contains historical recordings of its attacks, sightings, and a replica of its footprints. The spirit of Tsul 'Kalu has been seen and/or heard by many throughout the country in present-day sightings, especially in the Appalachian Mountains and in areas where there is a connection to the Cherokee tribe. I never thought I'd meet it, and I pray I never will again.

I gained a new respect for Lori's expertise and knowledge of the Cherokee nation and traditions. She told us about the sweat lodges, peace pipes, festivals, religious ceremonies, and war rituals of the tribe. It was not only interesting, but I hoped her enlightenment could help us find answers to the questions that plagued us and rid the land of these ghostly curses. Hopefully, sooner rather than later.

Lori was in the living room, burning sage, pouring salt around the doors, and explaining those traditions to Robin. The Cherokee believed that burning sage warded away evil spirits and cleared negative energy from the room. They also believed that pouring salt around the doors, top and bottom, kept evil spirits from entering. It sounded quite absurd to me, but I was willing to try anything that could possibly protect us from these monstrous wraiths.

It was 1:10 AM, and we could still hear the drumming next door. Tat-tat-tat. Tat-tat-tat. It was non-stop.

None of us had slept a wink, nor were we even sleepy. It had been a day of way too much phantasma, overstimulating, to say the least. And now, tat-tat-tat kept us wide awake, on our toes, and in suspense of the unknown and the unexplored. Tat-tat-tat was calling us.

"I think we should go over there and see what's goin' on," said Robin.

She'd paced the floor and looked out the window repeatedly for the last half-hour. I teased her about having ants in her pants.

"I've got a flashlight in my car," she said. "Whose comin' with me?"

"You're shittin' me!" I replied. "What if that creature is over there or comes back?"

I cringed at the thought of meeting Tsul 'Kalu again.

Lori spoke up, "The medicine man is there, and he will keep the Tsul 'Kalu away. I'll go. Maybe we can find out what the mysterious drummin' is guidin' us to, just like in my dream. The drummin' is supposed to guide us to... to... to somethin'. I'd like to find out what."

It was plain to see that I was outnumbered. I didn't want to go; I just wanted it to go away. *If I could just climb*

69

in bed, cover-up, and pretend none of this was happening, I'd be fine, I thought.

But it *was* happening, and ignoring it wouldn't make it go away. I was both afraid to go and afraid to stay. I finally decided it was best to go with them and face these spirits head-on rather than stay home alone and constantly worry about what they were encountering next door.

At least we'd have the support of each other, come what may. So, I fetched my 2 best flashlights from the utility closet for myself and Lori since Robin had her own. Two Powerful XLs, the brightest there are. Expensive, but powerful. Whatever was there, it couldn't hide from the light of the Powerful XL.

"I can't believe I'm lettin' you talk me into this," I said to Robin as we exited the front door.

"The sooner we go over there and check it out, the sooner we'll know what's causin' this madness," said Robin. I hoped she was right.

Tat-tat-tat was calling us, and we were on our way.

CHAPTER 8

The old house reeked of cobwebs, dirt, and grime and smelled moldy and nasty, as any old house that's been abandoned would. Sheetrock had peeled off and broken into a million pieces all over the floors and left gaping holes in the ceilings and walls. It was hard to walk without stepping on sheet rock or big globs of dirt and debris that had accrued there through years of wind and rain and mud seeping in through the broken windows and the leaky roof.

The house was small, with 4 rooms and a basement. You could stand in the hallway and see every room. A kitchen, living room, a bedroom, and a bathroom. In the kitchen, the trim and framing had been pulled apart, maybe with a crowbar, and exposed an open area where a basement door once hung. The basement stairs were totally missing, exposing a direct drop-off, about 6 feet, from the kitchen into the basement below it. I wondered if the floor was sturdy enough to hold us. It shook when we walked across it. I imagined it caving in with us and shuddered to think of the dangerous mishaps and calamities that could occur.

There was no furniture in the house. It was totally empty. Nothing there except us, the wraithy phantom drummer, and the obscuring smoke that surrounded us like vapor the minute we entered the house. The front door had fallen off its hinges when we opened it, so we propped it up on the front porch outside.

Then, SWOOSH. A cold wind gushed in behind us through the opening where the door had been. It was so strong I could hardly stand and so cold my breath vaporized and mixed with the mystic smoke around me. Had we opened the door to more spirits? It appeared so, or possibly the ones that were here, became stronger. The wind was colder, and the smoke was thicker, and tat-tat-tat was louder.

"Let's split up," said Lori. "If each of us searches a separate room, maybe we'll find the drummer sooner."

We went our separate ways, Robin in the kitchen, Lori in the bedroom, and me in the living room. Hopefully, it wouldn't take long for one of us to find a clue as to where the drumming was coming from.

Ironically, it sounded the same in every room of the house, so it was difficult to find where it originated. We yelled back and forth to each other periodically, checking on each other's safety and supporting each other in our search.

I surveyed the living room with as much scrutiny as I could without daylight. The smoke and the wind around me had created an upward-spiraling spoof that soon morphed into glowing figures twisting and twirling their way through the air as far as my eyes could see. I couldn't make out their forms, but I could see their blurred features whipping in and out of the smoke, disappearing and reappearing like they did in my garage, but with a lot more strength and energy.

They whirled around and back and forth, wavering in and out from one realm to another. Each time, their forms and features became a bit clearer as they gained more power to enter our reality. The whole room buzzed with a supernatural electrical haze that grew louder, more distinct, and more horrifying. The smoke was thicker, the buzzing louder, the swaying revenants more visible, and the tat-tat-tat sounded even louder.

The smoke continued to thicken. Now, it was so thick I couldn't see anything, even with my flashlight turned to its brightest setting. I couldn't see through the haze or anything beyond it. Just a thick, undulating maelstrom of smoke engulfing the entire house, buzzing with bodiless entities and their indelible oppression.

I was dizzy and starting to panic. I crouched into a corner and made the sign of *the cross* for protection. I closed my eyes and covered my ears with my hands. I didn't want to see or hear anymore. All I wanted was for the smoke to go away and the drumming to stop and for my life to return to normal the way it was before any of this happened. I thought about leaving and going home, but first, we must find tat-tat-tat.

"Are y'all okay?" Lori yelled.

"I'm here," Robin answered. "Still in the kitchen."

"Me too," I said, "I'm here in the livin' room."

At least we were all here together and safe, but it was obvious that *we were not the only ones here.*

Ebbing through the murky mist, I heard, "*We're here. We're here. We're here…*"

A choir of sepulchral voices, harmonizing and echoing, one after another. Eerie whispers close, yet far away, seething from the omnipresent ether. "*We're here. We're here.*"

Multiple voices, I couldn't count how many, but *they were here.*

Finally, the voices and the apparitions faded into the obscure dimension from which they came. Maybe they were still here, just invisible; I wasn't sure. At least for the time being, all was silent except for tat-tat-tat.

I was still crouched in the corner with my hands over my ears when Lori entered the living room. She'd brought the sage with her and was smudging the house and mumbling something in Cherokee. It must be working, I thought, because the smoke had dwindled and now formed a thinning mist that slowly dissipated upward through the ceiling.

"The medicine man is still here," said Lori. "When you hear the drummin', he's here. When the drummin' stops, *run*. As fast as you can *run*, and don't look back."

"Why?" I asked.

"You may think it's evil when he's here," she said, "but when he leaves, many more evil creatures like Tsul 'Kalu and others come around because there's no one to stop them. Just *run* as quickly as you can. *Run. Run.*"

She finished smudging the living room and searched every nook and cranny, I assumed, for more clues.

"I'd rather run right now," I said. "Why wait?"

I was half-serious, half-joking, but I knew we couldn't leave yet, though I wanted to go so badly.

"We need to find the portal first," said Lori, "and the drummer while he's still drummin'."

"A portal," she explained, "is a spiritual doorway or passageway where spirits enter and exit our reality. This house seemed to have several portals; we just needed to find them. Usually, a portal is an actual doorway of a room or house, or it could be a mirror or picture within the house. When you close off a portal, spirits can no longer come through."

She was adamant about finding it and believed that it was the only way to stop these hauntings.

Since there were no pictures in the house that left either a mirror or a door as portals, the mirror in the bathroom was shattered, and part of it had peeled from the wall.

"It was still possibly a portal," Lori said.

She smudged the bathroom with the sage, especially around the mirror, chanting in Cherokee.

"We need to come back when it's daylight," she said.

"I will talk to Uncle Jim about putting boards over these holes," she said. "I'll tell him everything."

"Great," I responded. "I want to talk to him, too, when he gets back in town."

She finished smudging the bathroom, and we were heading to the kitchen when we heard…

A scream, a crash, a thud, then silence… and tat-tat-tat stopped.

CHAPTER 9

"Robin, are you okay?" I screamed.

She didn't reply. "Robin!"

Nothing.

Lori and I both yelled her name over and over. No reply. Only silence. A morbid silence, the kind where you knew something had gone badly wrong.

The drumming had stopped, and Lori said when it stops, *run*. But we couldn't leave without Robin. My feet throttled into a full-speed malady into the kitchen with Lori close at my heels. We shined our flashlights in every corner of the kitchen and kept yelling for Robin.

No reply and no sign of her anywhere. Where could she be? We both knew that if Robin were anywhere in sight, she'd be talking non-stop. "Silence is golden," they say, but silence wasn't one of her virtues.

Maybe the spirit activity had been too much for her, and she'd gone outside to catch a breath of fresh air? It's unlikely that she'd go outside without telling us, but I felt we should search outside anyway, just to be sure.

My hand was on the doorknob when I heard a
grrrrrrrrrrr sound just outside the kitchen window. A
beastly growl. Fierce. Gnarly. The sound of a bloodthirsty
creature that would surely tear me to shreds if it got ahold of
me. I winced at such a horrid thought.

Hide Vicki, I told myself. *Hide quickly*. Lori had said
run, but we couldn't leave without Robin, so our only option
was to hide.

The only thing in sight were the kitchen cabinets, so
I crouched down and hid behind a cabinet door. Lori
crouched down beside me. We both shined our flashlights
toward the half-broken window into the dark, lugubrious
night. Its darkness stared back at us but not with its eyes. Its
entire being swaddled us like a massive blob of nothingness,
blocking the whole window and transmitting metaphysical
vibes of hate and danger and cruelty.

Our flashlights couldn't penetrate its blackness; we
couldn't see anything above, below, around, though, or
beyond it. Not even the moon or the stars. It was like an
eclipse of flagrant evil, overshadowing our view of light and
hope and sanguineness.

Run. Run. Run. The drumming had stopped. *Run* as
fast as you can because creatures more wicked than the

medicine man come around with no one to stop them. It appeared we had waited too late to run and were now trapped. The noxious spirit beast surrounded the house, and we had no idea how far its hideous antipathy spanned or what would happen if we embarked upon its trail. It wasn't safe to go outside, plus we still had to find Robin. Where was she? Why wouldn't she answer us?

I could still sense the monster's loathing enmity but refused to look up at the window again. I didn't want to give it any more leverage to further frighten us. It seemed to savor our attention and maraud upon our fears. I was determined not to let it, or Lori knew how terribly afraid I was. We had to find Robin, no matter how intimidated we were by its nefarious reign.

I retraced my footsteps through the kitchen, and this time, I saw it. How could we have overlooked it before? Part of the floor had caved in at the drop-off to the basement, where the door and the stairs were missing. Had Robin fallen through the drop-off? I inched my way there to find out, tiptoeing to be sure the floor would hold up beneath me.

I shined my flashlight into the basement and said, "Robin, are you there?"

I was close to tears and thinking about the worst possible scenario when I heard a moan and a whimper from below.

"I'm here," she responded feebly.

I shifted my flashlight in her direction. It was difficult to see her because she was sprawled out on the basement floor behind where the staircase used to be. Underneath her were parts of disassembled cardboard boxes and several strips of wall insulation.

On one side of her were 2 old bookcases, and on the other side, a wall with full-size built-in shelves where 5 large rocks, at least a foot long each, lay on the floor by the bottom shelf. What an odd combination of stuff to find in an old, abandoned basement, I thought.

It was also strange that Robin fell at such an odd angle. Down and backward and luckily on something cushiony without hitting her head on the floor or the bookcases, shelves, or rocks. It made no empyreal or gravitational sense, but at least she wasn't seriously hurt. She sat up, wheezing and clutching her ankle. I assumed the fall had knocked the wind out of her, and she was trying to catch her breath.

"Damn, we've been worried shitless," I said. "Don't ever do that again."

"We've got to get outta here," said Lori.

The easiest way to get to her would be through the outside basement door. But the beastly apparition still lurked around the house in full force. Its scintillant blackness sheathed every window and shrouded us with a webbed cocoon of ravaging hostility.

Going outside right now was out of the question. The only way to get to Robin was to lower ourselves down the drop-off into the basement, wait for the beast to leave, and then we could all exit through the basement door to go home when the time was right. But how could we get down there to her from here without injuring ourselves?

"I'm comin' down there," I said to Robin. "Push one of those bookcases over here so I can stand on it."

Robin stood up and limped to the bookcases and leaned on them.

"Not very sturdy," she said. "It might not hold you up."

"Well, push the 2 of them together," I said, "I'm comin' anyways."

"There's a pipe to your right as you come down that you can use to balance yourself," said Robin.

She pointed to the pipe, and I saw it in the shadow of my Powerful XL, which was starting to dim and lose energy. The pipe didn't look very sturdy either, but it was good to know it was there just in case I needed to grab ahold of it to steady myself.

Robin pushed both bookcases together under the drop-off and held them in place, and Lori shined the flashlight on me while I lowered myself onto them. It was a bit of a challenge balancing myself, but Robin stood ready to catch me if I fell, bookcase or no bookcase. Once I landed safely on the floor, I gave her a big bear hug.

"Thank God you're okay," I said.

We both cried. She was covered in soot and dirt from head to toe and still gasping.

I looked around the basement for a ladder, but there wasn't one. The only things there were a dingy old toolbox, an old, faded desk, the two bookcases under the drop-off, more insulation scattered about here and there, and the 5 big rocks on the floor below the wall with the built-in shelves.

Since we couldn't find a ladder, the only way for Lori to get down the drop-off was for us to help her down. I hoped the crumbling kitchen floor would hold up long enough for her to lower herself into the basement, but I couldn't be sure. We'd just have to take the chance. I grabbed her flashlight and heard a *grrrrrrr* much louder than the last one. It startled me, and I nearly dropped my Powerful XL.

In fact, *grrrrrrrrrrrrrrrrrrrrrrr* was all around us now. Everywhere. Like an omnipresent surround-sound stereo system blaring its mephitic verve from all corners of the cosmos... *all around you.*

Lori held onto the kitchen floor and began her descent onto the bookcases below. But she didn't make it that far. In mid-air, the flooring she held onto crumbled and came crashing down with her, and pieces of broken tile flew everywhere.

Lori squealed and grabbed hold of the loose pipe that Robin had told us about and momentarily dangled in the air with it until it broke loose and fell. The pipe hit the floor with a deafening clang, but we managed to catch Lori before she hit the floor.

"Damn," she said as she dusted herself off. "Got to watch that first step; it's a real bitch."

84

Normally, I would've burst out laughing, but the maddening growl from just outside the basement door reminded me that this was no laughing matter. The 3 of us scrunched together like bleating sheep awaiting slaughter behind the wall where the bookcases had been. My flashlight went dead, so I placed it on the 3rd shelf from the top of the wall behind us and used my phone light instead. Lori did the same.

Robin's flashlight was shattered, and pieces of it scattered on the floor next to my feet. The batteries had fallen out and lay on the floor at the base of the built-in shelves. I picked up the batteries and broken pieces and placed them on the shelf beside my flashlight.

At least we were all 3 back together again, finally, even though we were scared out of our wits. If we could just go home now, everything would be all right, at least for tonight. But it didn't look like we could leave any time soon. *Grrrrrrrr* was still out there, seeping through the darkness, watching, interposing, intimidating. We were stuck playing the waiting game until it left, and it turned out to be the most terrifying waiting game I'd ever played in my life.

We hid from the ghostly mass, but it knew where we were. We remained silent, but it skimmed our thoughts with its telepathic sensors and preyed upon our jaunted fears. Its grueling wrath was right upon us; this time, its growl was so loud and deafening it shook the whole house.

Grrrrrrrrrrrrrr. Grrrrrrrrrrr. Louder, stronger. I thought the whole house would collapse on top of us. Run… the drumming stopped. Run. The medicine man is gone. There's no one to stop the evil. Run. Run. Run.

I wanted to run so fast and so far away that no one could ever find me. Not man nor spirit or beast. But the house quaked with such vengeance that all I could do was hold on for dear life to one of the built-in shelves to keep from falling. An earthquake? No, but the thunderous grumbles from the wretched spirit beast brought an aftershock just as deadly.

We held on to whatever we could find, but the built-in shelves proved to be the most stable structure around us. The bookcases tumbled over, and the old desk turned sideways and hit the floor with a clang. Studs and pipes rattled like termagant hail clanging against a tin roof.

The floor above us shook unmercifully, like hundreds of lost souls swiveling underwater with a sinking ship. Huge amounts of broken tile crumbled through the drop-off around us. Did the whole kitchen floor cave in? I wasn't sure; I just held onto the shelves. We all did. And, like an anchor in the sea, they stood strong. If everything around us had crumbled, I'm convinced those built-in shelves would still be standing. *I didn't know it at the time, but they were the foundation of a lot more than just our safety net during that ghostly tremor.*

Finally, the house stopped quaking, but I was still shaking like a leaf. I had a sense of going round and round on a freaky carousel that wouldn't stop and let me off. I felt dizzy, nauseous, and helpless. Why wouldn't this thing just go away and leave us alone? I rested my head on one of the shelves and tried to center myself. It took a few minutes, but I stood up, and in doing so, I saw something else quite bizarre.

Carved into the wall between the shelves were pictures and symbols, old and faded but barely visible, 5 of them. A mountain, two sun symbols side by side, a Native American headdress, a square cross, and a picture of a diamond with a smaller diamond inside it.

"Y'all look at this." I pointed and held my phone light closer to the ancient drawings. Lori studied them carefully, squinting to see through the dim light.

"Petroglyphs," she said. "I know what these symbols mean."

"Really," I said, "tell us, tell us."

"The mountain means great adventure," she said. "The sun symbol represents happiness. The headdress means ceremony. The square cross represents life's journey. The diamond-shaped symbol means medicine."

"Wow!" I was flabbergasted. Petroglyphs? In the wall of the old basement? How did they get there? The structure wasn't old enough to house the original carvings of the Cherokee, but they looked original, faded, and barely visible. I examined them more closely, intrigued about finding proof of such a lamentoso yet important part of history.

Were there hidden messages in those symbols from the Cherokee to us for today?

"They live on," Jessie Flatte had said, and as crazy as he was, I could now see his point. They wanted us to keep their culture alive.

Intuitively, I knew there was much more to discover. But not tonight! I was too overwhelmed to handle any more ghostly culture shock. I'd come back tomorrow during the day, I was sure of that, to explore these findings more thoroughly.

"I'm surprised you didn't see these symbols when you fell," I said to Robin. "You fell right in front of them."

As I spoke, the darkness lifted. The air was lighter. Smoother. As quickly as it appeared, it was gone. The darkness and oppression were gone, and it was finally time to go home.

Robin had apparently hurt her ankle and was still limping, so Lori held one arm and the other so she could walk more easily without putting full weight on it.

"Well," she said, "I didn't fall, I was pushed."

CHAPTER 10

The old house was calling my name more than ever now. Like a lingering cacoethes in a whirlpool of astral diversion, it called… *"We're here. We're here."*

I'd embarked upon a paranormal fantasia with a mystique history and too many dark secrets for me to just let it all go. I was determined for the daylight to tell me what the darkness couldn't.

I barely slept last night, 2 hours at the most. Neither Lori nor Robin slept much either. We were way too keyed up to rest, so we recaptured among us the day's events in the woods and at the old house. We concluded that some intelligent higher entity must've guided these events and us to the old house.

After all, Lori and I both dreamed that the "drumming would guide us to… to… to…" something, and we'd found the petroglyphs. But what now? Was there more? Indeed, there was much more.

We also shared our pictures, the ones we'd taken on our hike to the waterfall. That's when I discovered that I wasn't the only one who'd captured a picture of the mysterious flute player apparition. Robin did, also. Lori snapped 3 pictures in the forest of the smoke she'd seen, but they were pitch black on the screen like the ones I'd taken the first day I saw it.

The fact that Robin was pushed, instead of falling, down the drop-off to the basement limned a more ill-omened perspective to our haunted journey. She told us that she felt a hand on her shoulder blade that pushed her forward and lifted her onto the cushioned area where we found her.

That explained why she was lying in such an odd place and wasn't seriously injured. Plus, as soon as she landed there, the drumming stopped, signifying that this being was drawing our attention to the area where it placed her—the wall with the built-in shelves with the 5 big rocks below it, where we found the 5 petroglyphs. It was a lot to process but so strategically planned.

Robin and Lori had gone home now with some far-fetched stories to tell their husbands, who, I hoped, would believe them. Terry would be back tomorrow, and I'd fill him in and hope for the same.

Meanwhile, I could explore the old house while Jim was still in Oakridge. He and David weren't expected back until tonight, which eased my apprehension about being here without his permission. Lori said she'd tell him everything, but I wondered if he'd believe her.

Would he be angry with us? After all, we'd trespassed on his property—in the middle of the night, at that, but since Lori was his niece, maybe he'd be more understanding once she explained everything to him. I'd keep my fingers crossed.

What else was here? I wondered. More scathing emblems from ancient days of yore? Hidden chronicles in spirit form lamenting the story of an obliterated past? That's what I was here to find out.

What else was it about that wall with the built-in shelves, the 5 petroglyphs, and the 5 big rocks that were so important to this other-worldly being? I wanted to know.

Besides, in the haste of all the chaos, I'd left my flashlight, and I was here to get it. I would've come back anyway, though. There was no stopping me from finding out all I could about these native spirits and their messages to us. I was intuitively drawn. Compelled. Driven, like a forceful gale sweeping through a pyrrhic hollow.

Was the same entity that led us here last night leading me back today? Something was I knew it, so here I was exploring the old basement, alone. It was quiet in a spooky sort of way, and I had the heebie-jeebies just being here. I was prepared to run if anything creepy happened. I'd seen enough extrasensory activity yesterday for a lifetime and hoped I could explore the house without coercion from man or beast.

The first thing I noticed was a bright light shining near the wall with the built-in shelves where we'd found the petroglyphs. My flashlight. It was no longer on the shelf where I'd left it. Someone—or something—had formed a big circle with the 5 big rocks on the floor and placed my flashlight in the middle of that circle. The battery was dead last night when we left, and now it was fully charged.

A circle of big rocks with a light in the middle? Strategically placed there by some intrinsic master designer from the other side. It wanted me to see that big circle of rocks for whatever reason. Did this master designer like circles? Light? Rocks? Were any of those things significant to the Cherokee? Maybe this spirit was just playing a prank on me. Was it another wild goose chase leading me in a circle to nowhere, like the flute player at the waterfall had done?

I took pictures of the shelves, the petroglyphs, the rock circle, and everything else I could find in the basement. I had planned to examine them closely later today at home and use them to do some research this week online as well as at the library and the courthouse.

Then, I took pictures upstairs in the living room, the bedroom, and the bathroom, especially around the broken mirror that Lori said could possibly be a portal. Half the kitchen floor had caved in, so I didn't go in there but took pictures of it from the living room and the hallway. With the task completed, at least for today, I went home.

I spent the evening googling Cherokee history in White County and its surrounding areas, particularly Bear Cross Mountain. One website led to another. Medicine men. Flute playing. Cherokee language. Drums and dances and tribal traditions. Cherokee artifacts. Burial grounds. Religious ceremonies. Piece pipes. Labyrinths. Folklore. Legends. Myths. Monsters that threatened the Cherokee.

I scrolled through the pictures I'd taken earlier today at the old house and found them to be way more sinister than I expected. Several of them showed white glowing orbs on the ceiling and walls, particularly in the area where I found my flashlight surrounded by the big rocks. I couldn't make out the forms, but multiple circles of light, at least 100 of them, all different sizes, surrounded the rock circle and glared like little rays of sunshine peeking through a half-closed curtain.

It was quite intriguing, but not as intriguing as the pictures I'd taken of the drop-off to the basement. I just knew my eyes were playing tricks on me. What I saw, or thought I saw, was impossible, unbelievable, but so was everything else I'd experienced this week.

I held the pictures under a brighter light for a clearer view. I'd taken 5 pictures, one right after the other, and was baffled to see that each one was different. A filmy vapor appeared in the background of them all, but in the doorway, there was something, or someone, different in each one.

One showed the doorway completely black. Another showed a huge glimmering light in the doorway like the one I'd dreamed about. A third one looked like a group of spirits hovered together, entering the kitchen from the basement drop-off. The 4th picture showed our mysterious flute player and the spirit beside him playing a drum. Tat-tat-tat.

The 5th picture revealed an image of a Cherokee man wearing a black bear mask with horns and 2 red dots for eyes. The spirits seemed to welcome his appearance with an afeared respect. *Obviously, I'd found the drummer, the medicine man, and the portal.*

I researched Cherokee tribal masks and discovered that they wore ceremonial masks to connect and communicate with the spirit world. But the medicine man's mask was different and believed to ward off evil spirits, heal those whom he thought worthy, and cast voodoo spells on those he wished to curse. He was both a blessing and one's worst nightmare.

I saved the links to the websites, typed all the pertinent information I found in essay form, and inserted corresponding pictures so I could easily find everything I needed all in one booklet. I named the booklet *Haunted Journal*.

Finally, around 3:00 AM, and even after 4 cups of coffee, I fell asleep. I didn't rest well, though; my mind was still charged both by the caffeine and my own officiousness, but my body demanded rest. During the night, I thought I heard the somber tones of the flute playing.

Hoooo-oooh-oooh-oooh-oooh-waaa.

Hoooo-oooh-oooh-oooh-oooh-waaa.

Dismal, yet mollifying. Idiosyncratic, yet restful. Soothing. Lugubrious. I'm still not sure if it was a dream or if it was real, but I drifted in and out of sleep while it played over and over in my subconscious… repeatedly stuck on, "*We're here. We're here.*"

I was wide awake and at the White County Library by 9:00 AM, analyzing historical reports and books about Cherokee traditions, rituals, and beliefs. I took my time and explored all the references I could find. I made notes and added information to the *Haunted Journal*. I checked out 4 books relevant to my fact-finding expedition to study at home. I also went to the courthouse and made copies of correlating archives to take with me to study later.

I brought home enough information to keep me busy reading for at least a month. The challenge now was finding enough time to thoroughly examine all of it. It was 2:18 PM. Terry would be home in less than 2 hours. *I may as well start now*, I thought, and buried myself in more research until…

"Honey bunny, I'm home." Terry barreled through the front door, smiling and rolling his suitcase behind him. Keefer jumped on him, wagging his tail excitedly, and nearly knocked him over; he'd missed him, too.

"I've got something to show you," said Terry.

He was tall, about 6'2", both muscular and stocky, and his jet-black hair was windblown and tangly.

"Here, check this out." He opened the photos on his phone.

"What do you think of this?"

He held his phone up in front of my face and repeated, "What do you think? Check it out. Check it out."

He was fidgeting, jumpy like a little kid bobbing up and down on the monkey bars. He scrolled through 5 pictures on his phone, all totally black. Wide-eyed and perplexed, he shrugged his shoulders as if to say, "What the fuck?"

"Well," I said matter-of-factly, *"you're about to meet the medicine man."*

CHAPTER 11

Marioochi's pizza was great, as always. Ciao Ryan was our favorite because it had every meat imaginable on it—pepperoni, sausage, hamburger, salami, plus onions, green peppers, and mushrooms. We ate outside so we could hear the bluegrass band playing in the outdoor amphitheater. The town square was full of mostly local folks who were shopping, laughing, dancing, and conversing with one another. Terry was on his 5th Coors, so I knew I'd be the designated driver home.

It was a pleasant evening, about 75 degrees and sunny, and Terry and I had a lot to talk about. I told him what had happened the last week, and he listened intently but maintained a calm poker face. I could tell he was processing everything I said openly but also with a lot of skepticism.

His response, as I expected, was, "Well, there's a logical explanation somewhere. Things like that don't just happen."

Then, he added, "That's fucking weird though. Maybe David or Jim was burning something on the property somewhere, and the smoke accumulated there above the garage."

I listened as he tried to find other logical explanations for these adverse events. He was innately analytical, and "facts" and "data" to back up all claims were crucial to his acceptance of any situation.

Keenly astute and shrewd, he was very detailed in his work and could fix anything that broke, but convincing him that something he couldn't explain or fix was real was a difficult task. *But soon, he'd find out for himself.*

"Pardon me, ma'am," someone said.

I turned to face a man who looked to be in his mid-40s, medium height and build, with sandy brown hair and a neatly trimmed beard.

"Yes?" I responded.

"My name is Rob Ellington," he said. "Forgive me for interrupting, but I saw you at Fall Creek Falls the other day when that old man went berserk."

"Oh dear," I said, embarrassed at the memory of that terrible encounter with Jessie.

"The old man made quite a commotion," he said. "But he's right about the property. It's haunted. I've been there and seen that smoke y'all talked about."

"Really?" I spoke.

"Yes, ma'am," he replied. "If you have a few minutes, I'd like to tell you my experience there?"

I looked at Terry, and he nodded his approval, so I said, "Please, sit down."

Rob shook hands with us both, then sat down in a chair between us.

"Me and my buddy, Jeremy Hopkins, went huntin' one day in those woods," he said. "David had said it was okay for us to do so. But we started hearin' some strange music and somethin' growlin'. We couldn't get outta there quick enough, and we saw that smoke y'all was talkin' about on our way out."

"Really?" I said, finishing my 2nd and last piece of pizza.

"Yes, we was pretty shook up," he said, "but curiosity got the best of us, and Jeremy and I both are now paranormal investigators."

"Well, that's mighty interestin'!" I responded.

"I figure we should try and help folks solve these problems rather than run from them," he said. "And I just wanted to offer our services to you."

He handed me a business card with his name, website, email address, and phone number on it. I stuck it in my shorts pocket.

"We've been interested in investigatin' that property for a long time," he said, "and was wonderin' if you could tell us how to get in touch with the owner of that old house. We knocked on his door several times, but he never answered."

"Jim Hartwell is the owner," I replied. "I don't know his phone number, but I'll be happy to give him your information."

"I'd appreciate that," he said.

"A lot more has happened since that day at the falls," I told him.

"If you don't mind, I'd like to hear about it," he said.

Terry bought him and Rob a round of Coors while I shared my story. Rob listened intently and reiterated his desire to investigate the old house and to help us.

We also talked about various topics—the White County fair coming to town, the upcoming Fiddlers' Jamboree in Smithville and the Big Foot Festival in Crossville in mid-October, new restaurants nearby, and other small-town talk. We all agreed to keep in touch; then, Rob left to join some other townspeople for more festivities in the square.

There were vendor kiosks set up all along the square, with people selling art, jewelry, jellies, jams, and other items of interest. I bought a jar of honey from Jon Cason, a local tradesman who owns Cason Meadows just west of Algood. I also bought some CBD gummies from Connie, my art buddy and owner of The Hemp Market in town. I hadn't seen her in about a month, so we chit-chatted and agreed to meet at The Art Shop and paint soon.

She said she and Bill were getting a divorce, and meeting to paint would be a great outing to keep her mind off things. I assured her I'd call her soon to set up a paint date and asked her to call me if she needed anything or just wanted to talk.

Then, as I perused through the other booths, I saw him in the distance at the outdoor amphitheater... Jessie Flatte. I nearly panicked, hoping he didn't see me. I didn't want another confrontation like the one at the falls a few days ago. I pointed him out to Terry, who agreed to handle the situation if he came near us.

"Well, what do you think of our talk with Rob?" I asked Terry when I was sure we were well hidden out of Jessie's sight.

"I don't know," he said. "We'll see. I say it's time to go home and have a drink."

I laughed. "Not so fast, mister, I think you've already had quite a few drinks. And we ain't leavin' 'til you dance with me."

I placed my purchased items on a nearby table, grabbed his hand, and swayed into the 2-step, my favorite old mountain dance. We danced for about an hour, then sat down to rest.

Before going home, we decided to take one last look through the vendor booths to see if we wanted to buy anything else. We found a vendor that did beautiful woodwork, mostly of patriotic symbols. Terry bought a wooden flag, and I picked out an eagle and a carving of the Liberty Bell.

We headed back to our car with our merchandise. Terry, still slightly tipsy, hopped into the passenger's seat of the Mustang and closed the door. I opened the trunk and placed our purchased items inside when I felt a tap on my shoulder, and someone called my name.

It startled me, so I jumped, and when I saw who it was, I was even more startled and angry. It was Jessie Flatte.

"What the hell do you want?" I said indignantly. Terry saw the encounter and rushed protectively to my side.

"I-I just wanted to apologize," said Jessie. "My behavior at the falls the other day was out of line, and I'm very sorry."

I wasn't sure how to perceive his apology, but he was in calm mode, so I relaxed a little but said nothing. Terry placed his arm around my shoulder and gave him a threatening stare.

Jessie kept talking and seemed sincere, but I didn't want to hang around long enough to see if his out-of-control mode kicked in again. He offered to fix our air/heating unit for free the next time something went wrong with it and handed Terry a gift card for free service. Terry accepted the gift card; we both thanked him and then headed home. We played a few games of 8-ball on our new pool table.

Afterward, we drank some wine; one thing led to another, so we spent the rest of the night making love, laughing at silly stories, planning excursions for our September cruise, as well as some remodeling plans for our downstairs. I fell asleep in his arms; it must've been at least

2:00 AM, and I felt the safest I had felt in weeks since all the paranormal activity had begun.

We both slept until around 9:00 AM. Another dawning day, and everything started out pleasantly, but it wouldn't stay that way for long. In fact, I woke up with an uncanny feeling of being watched. I hated that feeling but had grown accustomed to it in the last few weeks. It was as though something had an all-seeing eye in every corner of the house and stalked me from room to room with debilitating subliminal reminders of *"We're here."*

Terry didn't seem to sense it and was carefree and cheerful while we ate breakfast. He cooked our favorite, scrambled eggs mixed with onion, peppers, bacon bits, and cheese with toast and blueberry jam. He was an amazing cook, but sloppy, and left the kitchen messy, with dishes everywhere, dirty pots and pans in the sink, and droplets of food on the counters and floor. I cleaned it up, loaded the dishwasher, washed all the countertops, swept, and mopped the floor. With the chores caught up, it was time for my morning shower.

Terry jumped in with me, which led to a morning of playful kisses and caresses, passion, and sexual frolicking. It was great having him back home. I felt safer when he was here and fulfilled by a pleasant and leisurely morning so far.

Early afternoon, Terry left to go to the shooting range with David to try out his new Creedmoor rifle. They had a specific shooting place in the woods not too far from the waterfall where we heard the mysterious flute player.

Most likely, they'd be gone for several hours, so I invited Lori over. She readily accepted. I told her about Jessie's apology then showed her the research materials I'd brought home. I also told her about my venture alone in the basement and about the big rocks and flashlights. I showed her the menacing pictures of the flute player, the drummer, the medicine man, and the portal of spirit activity that took place at the drop-off to the basement.

Fascinated, she scrolled through one book while I read another. We both shared our findings, and I added more information to the *Haunted Journal*. I was particularly drawn to a chapter I found on labyrinths. I'd never heard of one, so I asked Lori what she knew about them. What she shared with me was identical to what I read in the book.

In Native American culture, the labyrinth was a sacred place and a sacred walk. It was often referred to as a walking meditation or a single continuous path that leads to a center, and as long as you keep going, you will eventually get there, like life's journey. The labyrinth was used to quiet the mind, reduce stress, calm anxieties, and enhance creativity and insight. It was a place of reflection to help one find answers and recover balance in life.

"Wow," I said to Lori, "I need a labyrinth right now; I feel more like I'm in a maze."

We both laughed. "I hope we can find a picture of one."

Lori googled labyrinths on my laptop, and I scrolled through more pages of the book I was reading. I found a picture of one and studied it carefully while Lori explained what she knew about it.

"The labyrinth was a huge circle of big rocks, with smaller circles of rocks inside it. Each circle of rocks inside the huge one became smaller until you reached the center," said Lori. "All the rocks were the same size except the one in the center, which was significantly larger than the others. Sometimes, tribes used a flame or light in the center instead of a huge rock. Walking the labyrinth was a sacred and meditative experience and was meant to be done in silent contemplation. You walked inside the circle continuously between the rocks, around each circle, until you reached the light or big rock in the center. When you reach the center, you find the answer to whatever it is you are seeking. Sometimes, a tribal member would play the flute to enhance the meditation."

"Look! Here's a picture," I said, holding up the book for her to see.

"Wow, that's beautiful!" she exclaimed. "My cousin, Cody Blackbear, told me about them, but I've never seen one. He's a full-blooded Cherokee and owns a Native American store in Crossville. I'll introduce you sometime. He's a wealth of Cherokee knowledge."

"Oh, I'd love to meet him," I said excitedly, ready to pin her down to a specific date. "I'd love to shop at his store. Maybe we can go one day this week."

"Yes, definitely," she said, "or just go in his store and tell him you're my neighbor. I think you'll enjoy talking to him."

I studied the picture carefully, and it struck me like lightning… the rocks in the basement of the old house. The spirits had placed them in a huge circle and put my flashlight in the center. Were they symbolizing a labyrinth? Why would they do that? Did there used to be one somewhere on the land years ago? Was this one of the traditions they wanted us to keep alive?

I searched more historical archives for answers. Indeed, historical records reported that a labyrinth existed on the property between 1820–1831.

"Look," I said to Lori, handing her the report. "There used to be a labyrinth here on this land. That's so fascinatin'. I wonder where it was located."

She had said it herself: "Sometimes a tribal member would play the flute to enhance the meditation while walking the labyrinth."

The mysterious flute player had led us around in a big circle deep in the woods near the waterfall as we followed the flute tones. Is it possible that what we thought was a wild goose chase was the encircled pathway of a labyrinth that existed here centuries ago? A circle of light. The walking meditation that the Cherokee held sacred. The flute player had guided us right to it. It made perfect sense. I could hardly contain my excitement.

I had to tell Robin. I dialed her number and then quickly hung up when I heard the back door slam shut. *Loud.* It was no ordinary slam. It shook the house, and a wooden clock above the fireplace mantle crashed to the floor, and the metal hands flew off. Next came shouts of holy terror from Terry and David.

"What the fuck was that?" Terry exclaimed.

They laid their guns on the coffee table. Terry plopped down in the closest chair. He looked pale and ashy like all the blood had drained from his face. I could tell he was trying to stay calm and in control but was failing at it miserably. I'd never seen him that scared before, so I knew something terribly shocking had happened.

David couldn't sit still; he paced the floor, back and forth, like a frightened man in exile awaiting execution.

"That thing was huge," he exclaimed. "We shot at it, and I know we hit it at least 4 times, but it kept coming at us."

He was short and thin with salt and peppered gray hair. His whole body shook. His voice was loud and shrill enough to drown out the shrillest of sirens.

"Dammit, we couldn't kill it, so we turned tail and ran like hell outta there."

CHAPTER 12

David and Terry both said they saw the smokey mist in the woods while they were at the shooting range and watched it transform itself into a giant minatory figure about 10 feet tall, with white beady eyes and long vampire-like fangs. It glided toward them in mid-air, chased them, sent them home in a tailspin, and made a believer of them in the paranormal. Especially since they shot it multiple times, and it kept coming after them.

The book *Creatures that Terrorized the Cherokee* described a similar creature as fast, unstoppable, spine-tingling, and the Cherokee's worst nightmare, a shapeshifter. Shapeshifters had the power to supernaturally change their physical form at will and could appear and reappear randomly in human, animal, or spirit form. They usually floated in the air rather than chasing their victims by running after them on the ground. According to history, shapeshifters often attacked and brought horror to the tribal villages.

Many of the villagers were found dead in their homes with expressions of terror engrained on their faces. Others reported sightings of monsters that chased or tormented them in both daylight and in their sleep. Some called it *The Creature that Wouldn't Die*; others called it *The Shifter of Time*.

"Legend or real? You decide," the book said. Terry and David both now declared it to be real.

I added this information to the *Haunted Journal* just as Terry barged into the living room, smiling and waving an electric drill. He was replacing some of the doorknobs in the bedrooms and apparently had an idea he wanted to share with me that couldn't wait.

"Hey, let's fire up the grill tomorrow," he said. "We can grill some chicken and steaks and invite some friends over for lunch and game time."

It sounded great to me but a bit odd. Terry liked privacy and seldom wanted to have get-togethers so soon after returning home from a trip. He usually preferred a few days of rest first and to get caught up on chores and projects. So, although strange, I agreed and planned the rest of the menu and the games to play.

"We should start early, around noon, so we'll have plenty of time," I suggested. "Who all would you like to invite?"

"The usual," he said, "Robin and Coy. David and Lori. I thought we would invite Jim."

"Sounds great," I said.

I was glad he wanted to invite Jim since I was anxious to talk to him. It was time to clear the air with him about the paranormal activity on his property. I was curious to find out all he knew and what, if anything, he planned to do about it and to find out what he'd experienced in the old house or on his land.

Hopefully, Lori will update him on everything that happened to us before tomorrow. If so, it would be less awkward to approach him about the subject matter.

"You know," said Terry thinkingly. "Maybe we should invite Rob and his paranormal investigator buddy Jeremy. Do you still have his phone number?"

Now, the pieces of the puzzle fit together. He wanted to talk to Rob and Jeremy about his incident with the shapeshifter. Since he'd experienced the paranormal firsthand, he was ready to investigate the hauntings.

Terry was a go-getter and prided himself on staying on top of things and getting things done quickly and aggressively. So, even before he explained his intentions for the get-together to me, I knew what he was up to.

"I think this is an excellent idea," I told him, handing him Rob's business card.

"Rob wanted to meet Jim anyway," I said, "so here's the perfect opportunity."

Terry called Jim and Rob. I contacted Lori and Robin. Everyone accepted our invitation and knew that the purpose of our get-together was more than just food and games. It was time for us all to meet and discuss these ghostly incidents and decide what steps to take next to rid the land of these spirits. I felt a glimmer of hope and a positive sense of direction for us and the future of the land, even though the paranoia was by no means yet over.

The next day, everyone gathered at our house around noon, introduced themselves to each other, partook in the feast we prepared, and had fun playing corn hole, pool, ping pong, and a few other games we had available. The guys had several rounds of beers, except for Coy. He reached for one, then Robin elbowed him in the ribs, so he drank 3 Diet Cokes instead.

Eventually, the conversation led to discussions about the hauntings. Lori had updated Jim on everything that happened the night she, Robin, and I went inside the old house.

He was quite concerned and asked us not to go back inside without him or his permission to do so, saying, "It's just too fuckin' dangerous, and y'all might get hurt."

He also told us he was considering several alternatives for what to do with the old house and would be in touch with us as soon as his plans were finalized. He sparked my curiosity, and I pried for more information, but he said, "Aint nothin' final yet, but I'll let y'all know as soon as I get it all figured out."

I'd just have to wait, and I wasn't good at waiting; I wanted to know now.

I shared the *Haunted Journal* with the group to update everyone on the latest ghostly experiences and the research I'd done so far. Finally, everything was out in the open among the whole group: no more secrets and no more wondering about who knew what or worrying about who would and wouldn't believe us. We'd all experienced something sinister and agreed to keep each other updated about future incidents and to notify the group about any future activities or investigations.

Rob and Jeremy talked further with Jim and David about conducting a thorough paranormal investigation of both the old house and their properties. They agreed, so Rob and Jeremy vowed to return tomorrow with their EVP recorders and EMF meters and spend the night inside the old house.

They also expressed a desire to camp out several nights in the woods near the waterfall where we'd heard the mysterious flute playing and near the shooting range where David and Terry had seen the shapeshifter. They agreed to record all their findings and share them with everyone. I felt an air of excitement and support in our group, and it was great knowing that I was no longer alone on this haunted journey.

Terry also talked with Rob and Jeremy quite extensively after everyone else left. I didn't hear their conversation but knew Terry would tell me later. Meanwhile, I was busy with my own inner confab, and decided to sneak away for a walk in the woods alone while they were conversing. Hopefully, they wouldn't see me leave, and I could avoid their lectures on how dangerous it was for me to go by myself.

Indeed, it was eerie, going alone, considering all that had happened, but something drew me there, back to the waterfall. I instinctively knew where to go, and the sensation was so strong I could've found my way there blindfolded.

In the woods, I mapped out what I thought had been the labyrinth based on the trail we followed when we heard the flute tones. It grieved me that such a peaceful, meaningful place was no longer there. What had happened to it? Why wasn't it preserved? Who would destroy something so sacred? I could envision it in my mind, but there were no physical signs that it ever existed.

Did the Cherokee take the labyrinth with them in their hearts when they were forced to leave here? After all, the labyrinth was more than just a circle of rocks. It was a walk of faith, the meditation of the soul, the hiding place, a place of rest, refuge, and rejuvenation. A place to find truth, balance, and answers amid the chaos of life.

Surely, it must've been the Cherokees' place of peace, their escape from the monstrous villains in the woods, the toils of daily life, and the heartache and drudgery of captivity. The Cherokee spirits were making every effort to let me know they were still here. *They live on, and so should their labyrinth.*

If the labyrinth brought them such peace, then why was this land filled with such massive unrest and upheaval? How and when did things transpire into such unfathomable disarray? What would bring peace to the land once again?

I asked these questions as I walked around the invisible labyrinth I'd mapped out. It started at the waterfall, then circled through the field and into the woods, then back to the waterfall. I wondered what the land looked like when the labyrinth was here so long ago.

Most likely, there was a clearing where the woods are now giving it a clean appearance, setting it apart from the rest of the land. I envisioned a huge circle of rocks, with rocks forming circles inside the big circle, each circle of rocks becoming smaller until you reach the center, as both Lori and the books had described.

I wonder what they used in the center of the circle. A much larger rock? A flame of some sort? A Cherokee emblem? Walking the labyrinth was to be done in silent contemplation, with intention, meditatively, and when you reach the center, you find the answer to what you're seeking.

What was I seeking here in this labyrinth that I could only feel in my heart and envision with my fifth-dimensional eye? How to stop these dreadful hauntings? How to restore peace to this mangled land and our lives here on Bear Cross Mountain? What part was I to play in this harrowing journey of restoration and requital? What did any of this have to do with me? I didn't seek these paranormal invasions; they'd sought me.

I continued my walk around the envisioned labyrinth and took pictures along the trail, at least 30 of them. I'd look at them later and add them to the *Haunted Journal*. It was warm but breezy, and as I circled the labyrinth a 2nd time, I felt the gentle wind nudge me forward like a spiritual propeller, a driving force from the astral plane above me. I felt blissful and enlightened like I'd entered a higher realm of being and a broader state of consciousness. All I did was walk… the labyrinth… in silent contemplation… seeking answers—a sacred walk like none other, and *I was not alone.*

It grew darker, but I had time for one more circle around the imaginary labyrinth and could still make it home before dark. Slow, meditatively, I took 2 steps forward and *poof.* The air shifted like a crosscurrent in the ozone from turbulence to tranquility. An energy exchange from sorrow to solace, fear to confidence, cloudiness to clarity, age to ageless. Time to timeless. Walking from gliding… floating up, up, up.

I was out of my body now and gliding above the labyrinth and all of Bear Cross Mountain in a timeless realm. I saw it in full view, the way it was when the tribe established it: the labyrinth and the teepees that comprised the villages on the land around it. Horses, cattle, man, and beast were co-existing in the same harmonious habitant beside the stream and waterfall, through the valley, and across the mountain.

Together, there were 5 villages, and they all surrounded and were connected to the labyrinth. There was a short walkway from the labyrinth to each village so that each village had easy access to it. Their lives, their villages, and all their activities centered around the labyrinth and its sacredness.

I saw the area where my home and the old house next door now stood, the medicine man's quarters where he practiced healing and voodoo. I saw the burial grounds, the smoke signals, the sweat lodges, and the tribal dances.

In the essence of this non-physical plane, I saw it all, including myself, walking the labyrinth with members of the tribe. Yes, I saw them and me, all walking together somehow. I watched us from the heavens like a ubiquitous eyewitness gazing from an immutable existence of deathlessness.

We all walked together silently in a single file line. No one talked, but everyone displayed an aura of unity, acceptance, respect for one another, Mother Earth, and the power of the labyrinth. Then I heard the flute.

Hoooo-oooh-oooh-oooh-oooh-waaa.

Hoooo-oooh-oooh-oooh-oooh-waaa.

The flute player stood in the center of the circle, enhancing the meditation with flute tunes of self-reflection, light, and inspiration. Alpha and theta frequencies soothe a troubled mind and console a burdened soul. I felt a special connection with the flute player and realized that he was the one who had guided me to the old house, the 5 petroglyphs, the 5 rocks, the waterfall, and the labyrinth on which I now walked. He was my teacher.

Our eyes met, and he looked beyond me, deep into my soul. I felt his love and compassion as he relayed messages of his plans for the land to me telepathically. A plan he was never able to fulfill because of what he would show me next. *This is why we are still here,* he said with his extrasensory conveyance.

In that moment, he also became my protector because what he showed me next was so horrifying; I'd never have watched it if he hadn't revealed to me his purpose. *This is why we are still here…*

Darkness whipped across the sky like a toxic malaise and enveloped all 5 villages with an impending doom for miles and miles as far as the eye could see… only my eyes were eternal, and I saw it all, from start to finish.

There were screams and warnings, and the villagers took cover wherever they could find it. Some hid in their homes, others in trees or ditches. Some even hid in caves or crevasses beneath the ground. Anywhere there was a place to hide, they hid to protect themselves and their young. There was no warning and no time to do much else.

Smoke signals twirled upward from the medicine man's quarters, warning the tribe of the menacing danger ahead. Prepare to hide or prepare to fight. And then… tat-tat-tat. The warrior's drum, the heartbeat of the Cherokee, beat in a steady rhythm to the sound of marching soldiers who brought with them a floodgate of terror.

I watched in horror as a militia of about 30 men dressed in blue rounded up the tribe like they were a herd of cattle unfit for a trough or too lowly for the ground beneath their feet. Some were handcuffed or roped; those who resisted were shot or slaughtered and left to die in bloody ditches. Men, women, and children alike, begging for their lives amid the gut-wrenching massacre.

The militia set fire to the 5 villages, destroying homes, lives, land, traditions, and the last bit of hope among the tribe. Survivors were forced away from their hallowed sacrosanct into an unknown wilderness of despair and drudgery, and the land was cursed with the sting of death, sorrow, and mourning. Some wept. Some screamed. Others bellowed with deep heartache and pain like I'd never heard before. The soul's groaning, and the spirit's wailing at the onslaught of such a cruel and senseless genocide.

The flute player was among those who refused to go; he and a few brave others kept walking the labyrinth. Tears in their eyes, they walked forward, unwavering, steadfast, and untouched by the insufferable agony brewing in the nearby villages. I walked with them, proudly, in the sacred circle of life surrounded by the bitter shroud of death.

The militia fired more gunshots, now targeting the labyrinth and those who kept walking there and refused to be held captive. Slowly, each one fell to his death. Gunshot after gunshot. One by one, they fell, buried in the aftermath of the putrid gunpowder, the sulfurous smoke, and the bloodshed at the hands of the militia. The flute tones... faded and were no more. The flute player was gone, but even as I watched his untimely death take place, I heard his spirit telepathically say to me, "*We live on…and this is why we are still here.*"

Then, the militia gathered the rocks that comprised the labyrinth and tossed them into the nearby streams and lakes. Laughing and mocking, they set fire to the labyrinth as well as everything in and around it… and the labyrinth was no more. Then, I saw the rebuilding that took place after the Cherokee were gone, the transformation of the reservation to what it became and what it is now… but in the now, I saw the labyrinth restored.

Then… the energy shifted again… from timeless to time, ageless to age, omniscience to the limitations of the physical realm. Here I was, back in my body now, wavering between the quiddity of two obscure worlds, both of which now haunted me.

My heart was heavy, but despite the anguish, I felt a heightened perspective of empathy and power and a strong urgency to keep walking the imaginary labyrinth. I was still here in the body. In fact, my body never left; it kept walking the labyrinth. My spirit simply rose above the part I couldn't see to obtain a higher understanding of what I didn't know.

Everything was different now; my whole outlook on the land and the spirits had changed, and still, I was not alone. Glowing figures swayed all around me, in total silence in a single file line, some in front of me, others behind.

They filled the whole imaginary labyrinth, the same beings I'd just seen in my non-physical existence, only now they were in spirit form, glistening and shimmering like vibrant ebbing lights flowing around in the circle that brought them light. They were walking with me in my reality the way I'd walked with them in theirs.

The same beings I'd seen in the twirly circles in the garage and in the old house in the smoke. Only this time, I felt the same unity and respect among them that I'd felt in my vision. I still couldn't see a physical labyrinth, but I felt its power, and these beings walked with me in the circle as though the labyrinth was still there. I followed them; they were outlining it for me, revealing to me where the labyrinth had been. *We're here. We're here.*

The flute tones were playing again, and they were the same in both realities, only in this reality they didn't stop. Calming, consoling, bringing hope and illumination.

Hoooo-oooh-oooh-oooh-oooh-waaa.

Hoooo-oooh-oooh-oooh-oooh-waaa.

No, I was not alone, but I was not afraid! I was about halfway around the envisioned labyrinth for the 3rd time, but long before I reached the center, *I knew what I must do. I had the answer.*

CHAPTER 13

I couldn't stop thinking about my vision, the beauty of the land and the tribes who'd dwelt there, nor the horror of their obsolescence. I now believed that the 5 big rocks in the basement represented the 5 villages connected to the labyrinth. The flashlight that the spirits had placed in the center of the rock circle represented the enlightenment that the labyrinth brought to the villages… and the flute player was the guide, the enlightener of the soul.

While it was still fresh in my mind, I sketched the labyrinth and the 5 villages onto a large piece of canvas paper the way I'd seen it in the astral plane. Later, I'd paint it with acrylics to capture its vividness, but for now, I placed the sketch on the top shelf of my bedroom closet. I'd show it to everyone later when I shared my plan. I also had a plan on how to use the 5 big rocks, so I knocked on Jim's door and asked him if I could take the rocks from the basement.

"Certainly," he said, "feel free to go get them."

Then, I asked him if he'd decided on his plan of what to do with the old house.

"Yes, partly," he said, "and I'll share it with the group soon."

"I have a plan to share, too," I told him. "Maybe I can share it at the same time."

"That would be great," he said, "I look forward to hearing it."

I felt an air of excitement and positivity about the future of Bear Cross Mountain. I hadn't yet shared my vision or my plan with anyone except Terry. I wanted to talk with David and Lori before I shared it with the rest of the group since the incident happened on their property, and my plan would involve their consent.

I thanked Jim for allowing me to go inside the old house and get the rocks. I hurried to do so, and to my surprise, they weren't there. Disappointed, I wondered who would've taken them. Rob and Jeremy had spent the night in the old house last night. Did they take them as part of their investigation? *I'll ask them tomorrow when they come to the house to share their findings with the group.*

The next day, they showed up promptly at 11:00, as planned, along with everyone else. When I asked them if they'd taken the rocks, they stared at each other, puzzled, and asked, "What rocks?"

I reminded them of the day I saw the 5 rocks with my flashlight in the middle, and they both reiterated that the rocks weren't there last night, nor did they ever see or remove them. No one else in the group admitted to removing them either.

Disheartened by this roadblock to my plan, I wondered who else would've taken the rocks? Did a burglar break in and take them out of mischievousness? They served no purpose to anyone except our group. Maybe it was the evil entities playing a sinister prank? They seemed to love doing so. Could it be the enlightened spirits? If so, why and where did they move them to?

I'd search for them later; it was time for our meeting to start, and I was anxious to find out what Rob and Jeremy had discovered.

Rob spoke first and shared the EMF activity they recorded from last night's stay in the old house. The electromagnetic camera captured quite a few apparitions, mainly in the kitchen at the drop-off portal and in the basement near the petroglyphs where I'd seen the 5-rock circle. Glowering figures and orbs floated through the smokey air with an eerie finesse and an unearthly veil. I didn't recognize any of them, but their features were too blurred and hazy to discern much of anything.

Jeremy shared the EVP audio recordings, which picked up 2 sets of apparitional voices. The 1st one lasted about 45 seconds and captured the drumming followed by chaotic battle sounds, then screams of pain and sorrow like I'd seen and heard in my otherworldly experience. The 2nd recording, though staticky, picked up deep, gruff, raspy voices saying, "These woods are ours."

I couldn't tell how many voices there were, but it was more than one for sure, and they sounded malevolent and vicious. None of us recognized the voices or recalled ever hearing that phrase before during any of our ghostly visitations. Maybe Rob and Jeremy would find out more tonight since they'd come prepared to camp out in the woods, more about these culprits who so aggressively laid claim to the woods.

Terry and Coy decided to camp out with them. Jim declined and quickly let us know that he was "too old for that shit" and wasn't comfortable sleeping anywhere except in his own "fuckin' bed."

He also assured us that someday we'd be "old and ornery as fuck, too," just like him. David told the guys he needed to go home first and do a few chores and pack some supplies and would join them later at the campsite.

The guys gathered tents, flashlights, sleeping bags, pillows, and a cooler filled with food, beers, and sodas. Terry asked me for 5 of the edibles I'd bought from Connie in the town square. I smiled and said, "Ain't beer gonna be enough?"

"We'll see," he said. He tucked the edibles away in his duffle bag and then joined the others outside.

"I'll get you some more of these, I promise," he said.

Since the guys were camping, Lori invited Robin and me to stay the night at her house. We both accepted. Robin left to go home and gather some clothes and toiletries and said she'd meet us at Lori's house in about two hours. Meanwhile, the rest of us walked with the guys into the woods to find their camping spot. We wanted to know where and how to find them just in case anything creepy happened, and we needed to check on them during the night.

On the way, I told David and Lori that I had something important to share with them privately. They asked me to follow them home after the guys chose their campsite. I was excited to finally share my plan with them and to tell them about my out-of-the-body experience at the envisioned labyrinth.

Jeremy switched on the EMF machine and searched the woods for an area to set up camp, preferably a place registering lots of electromagnetic activity. It didn't take him long to find it. The air suddenly felt cooler, and a crisp wind stirred the trees. The sky darkened, and the EMF detector beeped with such intensity that it made my insides throb with heat.

Painfully hot, it felt like a hot, cold wind of fire and ice seared right through me, scorching every organ in my body. Weak and shaky, I sat down in a camping chair to rest, but rest wasn't in the stars for me today. In fact, the reboant sound of crackling leaves and the brutal crepitating of tree branches snapping and flying overhead let me know quickly that it wasn't the EMF detector at all that had caused the burning sensation in my body.

It was… Rob's wild-eyed glower and frenetic plea of "Run" validated the danger around us that we all sensed and knew was coming.

"Everybody, run. Now." He waved his arms back and forth in a frantic flapping motion, signaling everyone to go on ahead of him.

Terry yanked my hand and nearly dragged me through the woods so fast I couldn't keep up with him. I tripped, but he caught me, hurled me over his shoulder, and kept running. Lori followed close behind us, then Coy.

David stayed behind a little way to help Jim, who wasn't very agile on his feet. Jeremy and Rob came last. They stayed behind long enough to switch on all their detectors, which now beeped so fiercely I thought they'd explode.

Shrieking, panicking, gasping, we ran like hellacious gusts of wind whooshing through a forbidden hollow at midnight haunting. We swooped through the woods, all of us, but none of us knew where to go. I happened to remember there was a big ditch ahead, large enough for us all to hide in. I yelled to Terry, "Put me down."

By now, both I and his shoulders needed a break from him carrying me. Plus, the ditch was hard to see, and I needed to search for it. It was about 5 feet deep and mostly filled with flowers and rocks, waist-high weeds, and sometimes a few garden snakes. Well hidden in the brush, it wasn't noticeable at all; you had to specifically know it was there. I'd fallen into it once on a hike and sprained my ankle, so I remembered it well.

"In here!" I yelled and pointed to an opening in the underbrush that led down inside the ditch. One by one, we all jumped in.

We were all accounted for, though shaken and horror-struck. Thick brushwood all around the ditch made it difficult for anyone to see us, but we could see clearly over the embankment through the tall grass and had a bird's eye view of the campsite. I watched in awe the maniacal commotion taking place there. Branches flung every which way.

Trees fell, at least 3 totally uprooted, split into pieces, and pitched through the air like weightless time bombs detonating in space. Banging. Clanging. Snapping. Crackling.

Then I saw them, hovering above the campsite... at least 10 large black orbs. They measured at least 36" in diameter. They were circular shaped but twisted into different forms as they moved, short in stature but mighty in strength.

Distorted, gremlin-like creatures, they hurled themselves through the air with supersonic speed and force, barreling right through targeted objects shattering everything in their deadly pathway. Their attacks were deliberate, sadistic, ruthless, and next...

The guys hadn't yet put up their tents; if they had, it wouldn't have done them any good. The evil entities strafed right through the campsite and bombarded their supplies like a violent, stampeding mob of ruffians and left it in shambles.

The cooler Terry brought exploded, and the food and drinks inside it spewed through the air and all over the ground. Flashlights and tools flew one way while clothes, sheets, and duffle bags flew another. Sleeping bags and pillows were left twisted and torn and mangled by the maddening poltergeist pursuit.

Finally, the dastardly orbs pulsated into the woods above the trees and dissipated like toxic black vapor into a dark cloud above the campsite. Their voices growled angrily from the etheric fog, "These are our woods. These are our woods. These are our woods."

It was the voices we heard earlier in the EMF recording at my house, evil eidolons claiming their territory and destroying anybody and anything they perceived as trespassers.

They were gone now. It was deadly silent, and I nearly choked on the stale, balmy air they left behind. There were no words to describe what had just happened or the devastation we all felt. Terry stood behind me, deadlocking me in such a tight bear hug I could hardly move or breathe. Lori crouched beside me on her knees and hid her face in her hands while David cradled her protectively in his arms.

Jim stood beside David, flabbergasted and confused. Coy, Jeremy, and Rob watched the phenomenon, stunned but intrigued, thinkingly, trying to process information that just wouldn't compute with their logical minds.

"What the fuck was that?" said Coy. "That was damn awesome but scary as hell."

No one answered him or said a word, but we all exchanged glances as if to say, "What now?"

Where would this wraithy journey lead us next? So far, it seemed to continually lead us farther into darkness and more setbacks. The campsite was destroyed, and with it, everyone's hopes and dreams of establishing a peaceful land among us.

Would Jeremy and Rob give up the investigation? I hoped not, but I could see it in their eyes; they were thinking about it. What about us? Should we give up and move somewhere else where we wouldn't have to deal with this paranormal delirium? Life would be easier that way, but could I simply walk away and desert my friends and allow the land to be overtaken by evil?

NO! I recalled my spiritual awakening at the labyrinth and the beings of light that walked with me in that dynamic circle. Giving up wasn't an option for me, not now nor ever. Had I not already experienced the labyrinth's power, I would've lost all hope. But now, in my enlightened state, I knew the woods didn't belong to those wicked imps or Tsul 'Kalu or any of the other diabolical creatures that had terrorized us.

The woods belonged to the labyrinth, and the labyrinth belonged to the woods, and *these woods were OURS.* It was time to take it back from these evil inhabitants and honor its original founders. I couldn't wait any longer. I had to share my other-worldly experience with my friends. It was time… it was time.

Finally, the sky brightened, and so did everyone's spirits as I shared my empyrean vision with them right there in that ditch. They listened, and I could tell it inspired them and gave them hope, meaning, and comfort. The evening sun radiated through the inky mystic air and cast an incandescent glow across the sky. It'd be okay; there was light, and it was shining upon us from the troposphere.

I showed everyone the pathway of the envisioned labyrinth and suggested they set up camp there. Still willing to go through with their investigation, they agreed, so we all pitched in and helped move their belongings, what was left of them, to the new location.

To my surprise, the paranormal equipment was still turned on and working. It had stopped beeping, but there were no signs of any damage that I could see. The infernal orbs had destroyed nearly everything else. Apparently, they wanted their voices heard badly enough to put on quite a shit show but left the equipment untouched.

The tents were usable, though the coverings that encased them were ripped and tattered. Rob and Jeremy started to work, putting up their tents. Coy and Terry left to go back to our house to gather more food, drinks, and other supplies they'd need during the night.

Terry hit me up for more gummies since the ones I gave him earlier were undoubtedly scattered in space somewhere with his duffle bag and all the other missing paraphernalia.

"You owe me," I said and reminded him that Connie's phone number and The Hemp Market website were written on a magnetic notepad attached to the refrigerator door.

Lori and David walked Jim home since he was over-tired and could barely move. His house was close by, so they promised to return to the campsite as soon as Jim was settled safely inside, and they were sure he was okay.

As I awaited their return, I noticed that the nearby stream trickled much louder than usual. In fact, we'd been here nearly an hour, and I just noticed it. I wondered if the sound of everybody talking had drowned it out earlier or if the mystic flute player was bartering for my attention again.

After all, we were right by the waterfall where I'd captured his picture in the selfie with Robin, Lori, and me. I didn't hear any flute tones, but this waterfall had beckoned me earlier to discover the labyrinth pathway, and it was beckoning me now...

I pointed out the site to Rob and Jeremy, which piqued their interest. They stopped working and joined me there for a clearer view as I recalled the events that took place there last week. They snapped pictures and took videos and decided it was a good place to hook up their detectors. On my way back to the campsite to help them carry their equipment, I tripped over... something. Stumbled and nearly fell, but Rob and Jeremy each grabbed an arm to keep me from falling.

"Careful there," said Rob, "that first step is a doozy."

"Clumsy me," I said with a giggle and an eye roll, embarrassed by my lack of coordination.

"Well, that's a pretty big rock you tripped over," said Jeremy. "I'm glad you tripped toward the campsite instead of toward the waterfall."

"Me, too," I said, "that's a long way down."

We all laughed. "Guess I should pay more attention to where I'm going."

I looked down at my feet and espied the footprints I'd embossed along the dusty trail and the big rock that I should've noticed long before now. Indeed, it was a big rock. In fact, there were 5 of them there in a big circle at the exact spot where I'd captured the picture of the flute player.

My search for the rocks earlier today ended in defeat, but now it appeared as though rocks found me, not by accident but by design. I'd stumbled into the center of the rock circle, which is where the flute player stood in his reality, playing the flute. I didn't choose the center; the center chose me. My teacher was telling me that it was time for me to learn to play the flute. I was the *chosen flute player for this reality*.

CHAPTER 14

Lori and David were in full agreement with my plan, which was to rebuild the labyrinth and the 5 villages, and not only offered their land for it but also their time to help build it. I shared the plan with the rest of the group, and everyone else was excited about helping as well.

David cleared the land with his tractor and leveled the hilly parts with a backhoe. Coy and Terry used their pick-up trucks to haul big rocks to the area. My plan for the 5 rocks that "found me" at the waterfall was to paint symbols of the 5 petroglyphs we saw in the basement onto them and place each one at the entry pathway of each village.

Lori, Robin, and I searched for other Cherokee petroglyph symbols online, printed them, and decided to paint emblems on all the rocks. Connie and Valerie from the Art Shop helped us with painting them since there were so many; of course, everyone ordered smokes and gummies from Connie, so she brought them with her as well.

She also said she was glad to be involved with our project and that it was good for her to keep her mind occupied since her soon-to-be ex-husband, Bill, was "contestin' the divorce and stallin' things just to be a pain in the ass." Robin gave her a business card and suggested she make an appointment with her for a massage to help her unwind and work the tension out of her muscles.

Valerie introduced us to her husband, Randy, who helped the guys with clearing the land as well as loading and unloading the rocks and putting them in place in the labyrinth. He fit in quite well with them since he was a plumber and an electrician and knew how to fix or repair almost anything. He also liked beer, fishing, moonshine, and deer hunting, which made him fit in even more.

Cody Blackbear, Lori's cousin and owner of Blackbear's Indigenous Arts & Crafts in Crossville, taught us more about the history and culture of the old ways and helped with designing the villages. He and all the other guys pitched in and built 5 canvas teepees for each village, 25 in all. Lori and David said they were thinking about using it as a campsite for those searching for a paranormal adventure and willing to spend the night in the woods at their own risk.

Nothing definite yet, just a thought, they said. However, Valerie and Randy expressed their desire to spend the night in one of the teepees, and so did Robin and Coy. Rob and Jeremy also decided to camp out one more night there since they wouldn't need to pitch their own tents to do so.

They all planned to build a campfire, make smores, have a sing-along, and be on guard for any strange activity meandering there. They took a little moonshine with them, too, the blueberry one. Terry and I joined them for most of the evening's festivities but returned home for the night. I gave an open invitation for those who stayed in the woods to call us and come to our house if anything wild and crazy happened. No one came or called, so I assumed the night had gone smoothly.

I bought a Native American flute from Cody's store, and he gave me a few free lessons on how to play it. He also made Indian tacos for the whole group, which became an all-time favorite of mine. The other guys bought all the ingredients, and he brought his deep fryer and made the frybread. I also overheard Cody invite Connie on a date to the upcoming Octoberfest in Crossville and promised to teach her how to do the polka. He also invited her to a pow-wow coming up soon in Smithville. She happily accepted both invitations. I hoped the outings would take her mind off all the heartache Bill had caused lately and be a new start for her.

Valerie invited everyone to the Art Shop for a paint and wine party and offered everyone a 25% discount if we found 25 people to attend. That was an easy task, so we all accepted and committed to the following Saturday at 7:00 PM except for Jim, who said it would last "way past my fuckin' bedtime."

With team effort, we rebuilt the labyrinth and replicas of the villages, and they were beautiful, just the way I'd seen them in the other world. The woods lightened and took on a more tranquil air as though a bright light rested upon it. I felt safe and protected and knew we were making progress toward bringing peace to ourselves and to the land.

I practiced playing the flute for at least an hour most days at the labyrinth around 5:00 PM, which was the same time my vision had taken place. Each time I practiced, I felt more confident, reposeful, and one with mankind and nature. It was as though darkness and terror could infiltrate the land everywhere else, but in the labyrinth, I was safe. It seemed that no evil could touch or desecrate it.

There were times I felt the presence of the flute player beside me, playing his flute in harmony with mine. I thought I saw him briefly shimmering beside the waterfall, but it was quick, evasive, and in my peripheral vision, so I wasn't sure.

However, I was sure that the labyrinth had cleared this part of the woods from evil, although other parts of the land still contained untold legends, dark secrets, and skeletons in the closets of the past that we would soon unfold.

I added more information to *The Haunted Journal* nearly every day, and it was thick now, about 150 typed pages with pictures. Rob and Jeremy continued their investigation and said they had a lot to share and planned to meet with us tomorrow, Thursday, at 5:00 PM at our house. I wondered what they could possibly share that would be new or different from anything we'd already experienced. More revulsion and loathsome wraith to add to the journal?

Although rebuilding the labyrinth resulted in an irenic state in the woods, it seemed the obloquy next door increased and lingered there with a territorial odium that was determined not to let go. The drumming continued, and I often heard screams and growls bellowing, mainly from the kitchen and basement areas.

Sometimes, light and smoky mist flickered through the windows, and bosky shadows cast eldritch spells above and around the house. Every now and then, I saw the whole house shake like what Robin, Lori, and I experienced there in the basement. It was quite scary, but I learned to tune it out and focus my attention elsewhere. I stayed away, yet its residual harassment was always there, and I couldn't totally disengage from its oppression. Perhaps Jeremy and Rob's new insight would shed more light on how to rid that part of the land from its writhing activity.

Connie, Cody, Valerie, and Randy were now a part of our team and showed up promptly at 5:00 PM along with everyone else. Cody and Connie brought pizzas, garlic knots, and Italian pies from Maroochis. Robin and Coy brought sodas and ice. I set up 3 large folding tables in the living room with folding chairs so everyone could sit down and be comfortable while enjoying the food and drinks. Jim, who was wearing a mask over his nose and mouth, stayed in the recliner, saying he was coming down with a bit of a cold and would keep his distance from everyone just in case he was contagious.

"Been fuckin' sneezin' all day," he added as he cleared his throat and made way for more coughs and sniffles. He also had on another coat in addition to his red flannel jacket to keep warm.

Jeremy appeared somewhat stressed as he shared the audio recordings both from the woods and the old house. I wasn't sure if his anxiety stemmed from the investigation or if he was just having a bad day, but he was obviously ill at ease about something.

His hands shook, and he looked fatigued. I assumed maybe he was a bit weary from the investigation; it had been quite taxing on everyone. He played the 1st recording, which picked up growling, drumming, then white noise, followed by a man's voice saying, "It's me. It's time."

He asked the group if anyone had heard the voice or the phrase before. Everyone shook their heads "no" except for Jim, who asked to hear the recording again. He moved closer to the speaker and listened intently, then asked to hear it a 3rd time. "It's... it's...," he stammered.

Before Jim could finish his sentence, Rob chimed in, saying, "There's a video clip of this, too."

He plugged the detector into the TV and played the video for everyone. The video was taken in the kitchen of the old house. The background was smoky grey, as though there had been a fire, and all that remained were the ashes. Glinting through the smoke was the umbra of an old man wearing blue denim overalls and a blue cap. His ambiance was friendly, but he spoke sternly as though he knew the recipient would understand exactly what he meant by, "It's me, it's time."

Then, he disappeared into the smoke like the ebb and flow of twilight to midnight.

Jim, still stammering, pointed at the video and said, "It's... it's... it's my father."

Gasps of shock from Lori and David followed.

"Oh my God," said Lori. "I can't believe it."

"Earl Hartwell," said Jeremy. "I found out that my wife, Arianna, is related to him on his wife Beverly's side of the family, a distant uncle of some sort by marriage, I believe."

"Small world," said David.

Jeremy had told us earlier that Arianna wasn't interested in paranormal investigations but was intrigued by his discovery of Earl Hartwell's apparition since they were distantly related. Arianna worked as a hairstylist at The Cut Hut, which was located down the street from Connie at The Hemp Market on Spring Street.

She was best friends with Rob's girlfriend, Ginger Chaffin, who also worked as a hairstylist at the same studio. Both ladies were also nail techs, and I went there whenever I wanted my hair cut and styled or my nails done.

Rob had paused the video and enlarged the screen for a clearer view of Earl Hartwell's apparition. Jim's eyes were glued to the screen, and he now appeared deep in thought rather than bewildered or frightened. He smiled fondly as though captivated by a memory that he wasn't ready to let go of just yet. Then, he turned to the group and said with confidence, *"Yes, it's time."*

CHAPTER 15

Jim told us that his father, Earl, appeared to him in a dream about 3 days ago and told him all was well in his reality; it was Jim's reality that was suffering, and it was time to tear down the old house and let go of the past. Jim struggled with the decision to do so because he still had fond memories there, and it was the main sector on his property that still linked him to his father, other than the gravesite where his ashes were buried.

Seeing Earl's apparition on video confirming what he'd already told him in the dream let him know that, indeed, *it was time*. So, he made plans to bulldoze the old house to the ground and invited the whole team to watch and attend a bonfire afterward to "cleanse the fuckin' land and the old fuckin' house from its haunted past."

I was ecstatic; we all were so engrossed in Jim's plan that I almost forgot about the other clips Rob and Jeremy had recorded. They finished playing them. We heard more growling, drumming, silence, and a cluster of grueling voices, but I couldn't understand what they said. The video recordings captured an apparition of the drummer in the living room and a huge, dark, shadowy mass behind him that shaded the whole room.

Another video showed the spiraling smoke circle with ghostly chit-chatter that seemed to defy raspy growls and gruesome threats waning at them through the cosmos that repeatedly said, "We'll never leave. We'll never leave."

The gruff threats sent a chill down my spine, and an eerie but explosive silence penetrated the air like an ashy mold, toxifying the idyllic mood among us. Were these the same gremlin-like creatures that destroyed the campsite in the woods, or were there others? Yes, there were others, and we'd soon confront their cryptic fervor and bellicose melee in an all-out war for existence in the reality of our land.

Our meeting lasted longer than usual, and it was nearly 9:00 PM before we adjourned. I was excited about the bonfire cleansing but a bit trepid about the voices we heard on the recordings. We'd made great progress with the labyrinth so far; it transformed the energy in the woods from gloaming evil to a sublime paradise. I only hoped the battle to free the rest of the land wouldn't last much longer. What I didn't know was exactly how fierce that battle would be.

Before Jim went home, I asked him to preserve the basement wall with the petroglyphs before tearing down the old house. He agreed and said he had already planned to save it because it was an actual original old ruin from the Cherokee days.

Different builders, through the years, just placed extra wood around it to preserve it and make it sturdier. That explained why it was the most stable structure for us to hold onto the night the house quaked so fiercely. It truly was the house's foundation and ours during that time, and it would stand the test of time for many years to come. The next day, Terry and Coy tore out the petroglyph wall and placed it in our basement.

Two days later, we watched as the old house was bulldozed to the ground. The men set fire to the debris, and I watched with anticipation, feeling a sense of relief and the inspiration of newness. Letting go of the past and moving ahead with pride and purpose.

Jim called the bonfire "The Cleansing" and invited everyone to add any items to the fire they wanted to get rid of. David threw in some rotten boards from their back porch deck that he'd replaced. Terry tossed in some large cardboard boxes he'd planned to take to the dump. Randy and Valerie added some old canvases and art supplies from the Art Shop that were worn out and of no use. Cody threw in some scrap wood he had left over from carving wooden animals to set on display at his store.

Lori poured sage and bay leaves into the fire for extra cleansing. Connie threw in some hemp leaves to give the flames a little *"aroma."* Robin emptied a bottle of Jack Daniels she'd found in Coy's dresser drawer and threw it into the fire as far as she could throw it, and with way more vengeance than the fiery flames. Everyone's contribution to the bonfire signified that they were going out with the old and in with the new. A brand-new start—a new day in our lives and a new beginning on Bear Cross Mountain.

Cody brought a Native American Piece Pipe. Connie added hemp leaves to it and passed it around to all those who wished to partake. She reminded everyone that her contribution to the group was to heighten their senses and to help them live in harmony by providing the 3 Ps: Peace, Power, and Pot.

Jim wore a mask and stood farther away from the fire than anyone else. He told us that his bronchitis had worsened, and he didn't want to take any chances of the smoke making his coughing spells worse.

Otherwise, he looked confident, self-assured, and glad to be a part of the cleansing of his property. He still wore that extra coat over his red flannel jacket. Maybe he had the chills or a fever or an infection of some sort because it was way too hot for all that garb.

Jeremy and Rob hooked up their paranormal detectors at a safe distance from the fire and joined the rest of us at the property line, along with Ginger and Arianna, and they all took a puff of the piece pipe that Cody and Connie passed around. Terry opened a bottle of wine and poured a glass for those who wanted one, then proposed a toast to a fresh start on Bear Cross Mountain.

Everyone laughed, joked, got caught up on the latest small-town gossip, and made appointments for haircuts, manicures, pedicures, massages, paint parties, and social plans to get together again soon. Terry, obviously feeling a bit tipsy, serenaded everyone with some classic rock songs with his own out-of-tune, made-up words, some of which were a bit off-color, which made us all laugh harder.

The late afternoon sun dwindled behind a row of bright, puffy clouds that looked like huge cotton balls floating in the sky. With several hours of daylight left, all signs pointed to a warm, serene evening with clear weather, lots of fun, and no strange activity in sight. At least, I thought so until...

"Look!" Robin screamed so loud I thought my eardrum had burst. She pointed to the sky like it was some foreign object sparing no effort to demolish the earth.

"It's headed right for us!"

Shrill screams among our team blared so loud we nearly drowned out the fierce beeping of the paranormal detectors, which registered the highest possible activity on their monitors.

"Oh my God," screamed Lori, "hide."

But there was no time to hide nor time to spare as the massive black cloud twirled at airspeed and surrounded the bonfire in an all-out attempt to smother the flames.

We took cover in the garage and watched in horror from the windows. Huge black entities descended one by one from the cloud, hideous forms of different shapes and sizes, unlike any I'd seen thus far. They not only surrounded the bonfire, but as more of them descended, they shrouded the whole yard like a solar eclipse, shading the land from the watchful eye of both the astral and earthly universe. They switched from creature-like forms to blobs of black masses resembling huge tumor-like growths metastasizing their lethal venom, spreading from the bonfire into the woods.

Lori was first to leave the garage, yelling, "Tsul 'Kalu be gone. Tsul 'Kalu be gone." But not all of them were Tsul 'Kalu, nor did they leave.

Outside, the sky was pitch black in a whimsical pattern from the bonfire above Jim's house and into the woods, stopping at the labyrinth. The sky around the blackness was distinctly blue, as though someone had taken a black marker and blotted out a portion of the sky.

Hideous growls resounded from the bonfire, and I grimaced as I turned to see if anything was visible inside the now dwindling fire. I couldn't see anything, but the growling increased along with screams, screeches of pain, and abhorrent grief amid the aftermath of the entities' hellish descent.

"We can't let the fire go out!" Jeremy screamed as he and the other men made a mad dash to reignite the fire.

Only about one-third of the debris had burned, so there was still much to burn for the cleansing, although now it didn't seem like a cleansing at all. It seemed more like a dark fight for survival on a land that was cursed and doomed to paranormal degeneracy and reprobation. There were beings of light and beings of darkness haunting the land, and I'd seen them both, but now it appeared as though the darkness had overpowered the light. What was to become of us? What if the cleansing failed and the dark entities took over the land? What would we do? Where would we go?

The fire was blazing again now, and we resumed our festivities, though no one was quite as cheerful as before. I was on edge, looking around suspiciously, peering up at the sky, which was still hazed with the black-blue pattern that the entities had imprinted with their own malevolent essence. The growls and screams from the fire had faded but were still faintly audible above the sound of the crackling flames. Terry nudged me and asked if I wanted to go inside our house, and I said, "No."

The cleansing was for us all, and I couldn't be a part of it if I left, so I decided to see it through until the end, even though the end seemed nowhere in sight.

"These entities will not leave without a fight," said Rob as he approached the team. "We must focus our intention together. When they come back, and they will, we need to be ready. As a group, let's tell them to leave and declare out loud that we are cleansing the land of its dark past, and they are no longer welcome here. No matter what happens, declare it over and over. Don't stop. Persistence and unity will pay off."

I felt the wind pick up from the west as Rob and Jeremy double-checked their detectors to be sure they were working properly. They were beeping faintly, so we knew some sort of activity was in sight, though it wasn't very strong, at least not yet. We gathered in a circle, each of us relying on the support of the other team members. I felt the strength of our unified group as we focused our intention on the bonfire and its purpose.

The wind blew stronger and soon whipped through the trees like a whirling gush of polar air. I recognized that chill; I'd felt it before, and it was no ordinary wind. It was the grueling presence of something invisible but strong with vitriolic intent. The temperature must've dropped 50 degrees or more in a matter of seconds as it gained more strength with each twirl. Soon, it formed a pirouette of swiveling leaves, tree limbs, debris… and flames. As the wind swirled, the detectors beeped louder, registering stronger activity in the area.

Rob took the lead in chanting, "Leave now. You are not welcome here. We are purifying this land, and you must leave."

Everyone chanted along with him louder each time as the team gained more strength. Now we were chanting seriously loud, with all our might, and huddled together in a circle to keep warm, but I couldn't get warm even though I clung to Terry like bonded glue. The chilling wind pierced through every muscle in my body, like a cold knife stabbing each nerve right to its core.

But it wasn't as piercing as the hair-raising voices arising from the flames and pooling through the wind, "We'll never leave. We'll never leave. We'll never leave."

I couldn't tell exactly where the voices came from; they were everywhere in the wind itself. The wind was the voices, and the voices were the wind. They were one and the same, and there was no separating the two. Intertwined, voices in the wind skewed the airwaves with, "We'll never leave," followed by hideous growls and fiendish laughter.

The blackness in the sky started to stir again like clouds do when a storm is brewing; only this cloud had a guided purpose and only one goal in mind—to stop the cleansing of the land. It stirred its way back from the labyrinth, shrank in size, but grew thicker as it glowered directly above the bonfire. It hung lower this time, about 3 feet above the flames. It looked like a glowering battleship ready to attack, and that's exactly what it did. It grew blacker, but something underneath it was gleaming bright red, like a mixture of fire and coal smoldering in a furnace.

I wondered why it had stopped its pattern in the sky at the labyrinth, and then it dawned on me that it couldn't go any farther because of the protective powers of that mighty circle. What was in the labyrinth that halted its evil quest? Was it the rocks or the Native American symbols we painted on them? The silent contemplation and meditation that took place there? Was it the beings of light that had walked with me in that circle? Maybe all these things, plus the... flute.

Yes, of course, the flute! I rushed into the house and returned with my flute. The team kept chanting, keenly aware of the occultic warfare approaching us yet incognizant of when, how, and what to do to prepare for the coming onslaught. We braced ourselves for the worst... and despite my trembling fingers, I started playing the flute. I focused solely on the soothing flute tones, and the team formed a circle around me to signify their support.

Then, it happened... mass chaos. Deafening shots of fire detonated from the polemic cloud like lightning bolts onto the bonfire flames. Debris spread every which way and sparked flames in all directions. The flames spread like wildfire to the fence, the land behind our garage to the woods and beyond, and then...

I kept playing the flute. I closed my eyes so I could more fully concentrate on the notes and their power rather than the frenzied screams from the team as they scrambled to put out the fires. I tuned out the panicked wailing, the caterwaul of terror, the sound of the fiery shots, the crackling flames, the menacing growls, and the savagery of the pandemonium embellishing the land. I heard it yet detached my soul from it, and in my own telepathic world, I sent light, combated darkness, and declared the absoluteness of our reality with my enlightened mind and the wholeness of the healing flute tones.

Hoooo-oooh-oooh-oooh-oooh-waaa.

Hoooo-oooh-oooh-oooh-oooh-waaa.

I pictured the protective shield around the labyrinth in my mind and willed it to surround the land, every inch of it from the bonfire to our house, to Jim's house, to David and Lori's house, to the waterfall and beyond, and all the land in, around, and between. I envisioned the land inside an invisible bubble that was unshakable, untouchable, unbreakable, and free from harm and atrocity. I saw it fully cleansed, purified, fully flourishing with no disturbances, and free from all paranormal degradation.

The more I played the flute and willed my visions into being, the more the energy shifted. I transposed to a higher reality where I could imagine anything I wanted and materialize it into whatever reality I chose. I chose for evil to leave this reality and for the Native spirits and our land to be at peace in this reality and the next... and the next... and the next. I chose... I chose... I chose... and knew it would manifest.

In my mind, I affirmed, "Leave now. You are not welcome here. We are purifying this land, and you must leave."

The flute tones whistled through the firmament; they were one with the wind, and their oneness was sacrosanct. Our affirmations intertwined with the flute tones, and I saw them materialize in the ethereal world. *Persistence and unity will pay off...*

I'm not sure how long I stayed in my trance-like state, but when I opened my eyes, I saw something unbelievably horrific yet magical. I kept playing the flute... *and watched...*

CHAPTER 16

The fiery shots from the cloud had sparked fires everywhere all over the land, and at first, all I saw was massive flames and sheer hysteria among the team. Terry and Randy were combating fires closest to the garage with water hoses. Coy and David had gone to find other equipment at Jim's and at David and Lori's house to combat the fires deeper in the woods.

Meanwhile, Robin went with Lori to turn on the irrigation system in her and David's yard. Rob, Jeremy, and Arianna helped move the paranormal detectors to my driveway, away from the flames. Cody, Connie, and Valerie were pouring salt on the smaller fires.

Jim decided to go home and check and see if there was any damage to his house and said he would join us all later. Ginger, who had forgotten to bring her phone, yelled, "Somebody call the fire department." But I'm not sure if anyone did or not. If so, they never came, but there were others that came to our rescue. *Others… yes, there were others.*

Hovering above the flames, with a serene smile and an aura of bright white encircling him, was the flute player. I was somewhat surprised but elated; he'd heard my call the same way I heard his at the waterfall. Our eyes interlocked, and we both kept playing our flutes.

He appeared confident yet humble, strong, and unshaken. Behind him was a host of enlightened beings, and they began to separate and replicate into other enlightened beings and suspend themselves above the fires. There were hundreds of them, bright, shining figures of light. They filled the sky and the land with lights so bright they sparkled like glitter, much brighter than the flames and with much more zeal. As they ebbed above the fires, the flames slowly started to dwindle.

A host of enlightened orbs surrounded the dark cloud from which the flames had emerged. Their mystic energy emitted light as bright as their own essence, and the cloud slowly disintegrated into smaller pieces, melted to a misty vapor, and then vanished into the light of the orbs. The cloud was gone, yet the bonfire below it kept burning.

The enlightened beings continued to replicate and multiply. There were so many I couldn't count them all, but their intention was to rescue us and bring light. Some ebbed across the sky where the blue-black pattern had emanated; others continued combatting the flames with their telepathic sensors and their versant consciousness. They looked like thousands of bright, shining stars and planets encompassing the sky and the land and the fires, consuming them with their lustrousness.

The flames were only about a foot high now, starting from the bonfire into the woods. I kept playing my flute but followed the orbs; they were still gliding above what was left of the fire but appeared to be guiding the flames in a specific direction. The other team members followed my lead into the woods.

It was Rob, Jeremy, Arianna, Ginger, and me at first. Valerie, Cody, and Connie stopped smothering the flames with salt and joined us. Terry and Randy, who were combatting the fires behind the garage, were next to follow. None of us spoke; we just silently followed the orbs as though something magnificent was about to happen, and we wanted to be a part of it.

We passed by Jim's house; he was standing on his front porch watching the same phenomenon. He joined us in following the orbs and the slowly dwindling flames. David, Coy, Robin, and Lori were already deeper in the woods, where they'd been combatting the flames with more water hoses and the irrigation system, which was still running and soaking the ground immensely. They joined us in following the orbs and the fire, which was now only barely visible… to the labyrinth where the flames totally smothered out.

Still, no one spoke; we were all speechless and standing in awe of the multitudes of cosmic beings swaying among us. Pure light engulfed us from all sides: above, below, on the right, and on the left, enveloping us with the brightest and purest of light I'd ever seen. There was no darkness in the sky or anywhere that I could see on the land.

In fact, the light emanating from the orbs shined so brightly I couldn't even see the land; it was aglow with the radiance of oneness and spirit. It was like being in the center of a tunnel with no time zone, twirling with incandescence and shifting higher intelligence from the *"Unknown Realm"* into the known. Transferring omniscience from the Inner Circle to the outer and mystical preeminence to our mortality.

A group of enlightened orbs formed a dazzling circle around the labyrinth, and it lit up like a fluorescent light show in the photosphere. In the center of the circle, shining white with translucent light, stood the flute player, playing his melodious flute, emitting calmness and encouragement for all to relish. Even brighter rays of sunlight scintillated down upon him like glistening crystals forming a glassy bubble around him. I stopped playing my flute and watched him spellbound. The orbs wavered around the labyrinth and then glowered their way back to the bonfire. We followed.

To my surprise, the flames they had guided from the bonfire to the labyrinth formed a specific pathway between the two. The grass had burned, but the remaining dirt and rocks made up the perfect narrow trail, which they specifically and purposefully designed with a plan in mind. Why did they do this, and what was their plan? What were they trying to tell us? Was there a distinct connection between the bonfire and the labyrinth? If so, what was it, and why did they want a trail connecting the two?

The bonfire was burning low now, and nearly all the debris had diminished to ashes. The air was clear and felt lighter. The orbs and the flute player slowly levitated above the bonfire and formed the shape of a huge teepee.

"What the hell?" I spoke.

Everyone else looked as puzzled as I was, except for Jim, who stared thinkingly with a glimmer in his eyes and his lips pursed into a half grin.

The orbs slowly glided into the flames and were one with the light of the fire. Their celestial energy loomed above the fire and among us and penetrated the etheric air, every place the flames had been, and everywhere the orbs had blessed with their illuminating presence.

The sun was setting now; it formed a huge orange ball in the sky amid picturesque steaks of yellow, purple, and pink that crisscrossed above the horizon. The bonfire dwindled out, and the only thing left were a few billows of smoke teetering upward and disappearing above the trees. The cleansing was complete; the land was purged. I felt it, and so did everyone else, but we were still puzzled by the orbs forming the teepee shape above the bonfire.

"What do you think all this means?" asked Robin.

"I don't know," said Coy.

"I have no idea," said David.

Jim spoke up amid the bewilderment and said, *"I know…"*

CHAPTER 17

Jim knew for sure. His plan to build *"The White County Museum of the Cherokee"* was underway in no time, with the whole team pitching in. It was a large structure made of stucco and shaped like a huge teepee, just as the spirits had shown us when they levitated above the bonfire. David, Coy, Terry, and Cody utilized their carpentry skills to build it.

Randy took care of the plumbing and electrical wiring. Terry cashed in his gift card for a free heating/air unit with none other than Jessie Flatte. So, Jessie installed it, never complained, or got kooky at any time while doing so. Since he'd managed to stay in calm mode, we thought it safe enough to invite him to the grand opening of the museum.

It took nearly 8 months to fully complete the building since the winter months slowed down construction due to a lot of rain and snow. With everyone working diligently, the opening day finally came—March 4, 2024.

All the team members were there. Jessie accepted our invitation and came and brought a lady friend, Donna Kiser, a retired high school algebra teacher, who seemed to be the perfect balance of patience and candidness to keep him in line whenever he started to get a little high-strung.

Jessie had also helped us spread the word about the museum in town, so lots of townsfolk from Sparta and other nearby small towns showed up. We served turkey and cheese sandwiches, potato chips, cashews, cookies, and pomegranate punch and had a festive time greeting people and explaining to everyone what the museum was all about. We crowned Jim with an Indian headdress and honored him as the museum's founder, followed by the cutting of a huge white cake with white icing decorated with different colored Cherokee emblems on it. The amount of interest from people was phenomenal, and so was the excitement they created.

In the entryway stood a podium with a guestbook on top for guests to sign their name and city and state where they were from. Beside it was a desk with a glass case underneath where I kept the original *Haunted Journal*. It was complete and updated with pictures and facts from the first day I'd seen the mysterious smoke until the bonfire cleansing. A copy of it was displayed beside the guestbook, and for $50, they could purchase a bound copy with color pictures to keep.

Inside the teepee structure were 4 rooms. The museum comprised 3 of those rooms and featured walls with pictures plus life-size statutes and a write-up of the flute player, the drummer, the medicine man, and the enlightened orbs.

There were also pictures and statues of the diabolical orbs and creatures we'd run across, historical facts posted about them, and personal testimonials of people who experienced their wrath. They could purchase a book with that information for $25; the book was called *Haunted Creatures Among the White County Cherokee.* We also displayed the petroglyph wall with the shelves from the basement in the museum, which captivated the interest of historians, especially those of Cherokee descent.

A large hallway connected the 3rd and 4th rooms. On one side were the restrooms and vending machines containing sodas and snacks. On the other side was a gift shop called "*Cherokee Gifts.*" Cody, Connie, and Robin made most of the items there to sell, things such as flutes, piece pipes, wooden statues of teepees, drums, wolves, dream catchers, sage, bay leaves, pottery, and other Cherokee artifacts.

We referred to the 4th room as the Gozho Room, which means beauty, balance, and harmony. It was available for people to reserve for $150 per day or night for events such as weddings, receptions, business meetings and get-togethers, classes, lectures, and other social events. I committed to teaching a yoga class there every Wednesday and Saturday and charged $10 per person or $35 for an unlimited monthly package of classes.

Robin used her sculpturing talent to make the statutes and her sewing expertise to make clothes for some of the statutes. Valerie, Connie, and I painted Cherokee emblems on the walls for decoration and outlined facial features on the statutes.

Ginger and Arianna painted their nails. I also finally painted the drawing I'd made of the labyrinth and the villages, which I'd tucked away in the top of my closet right after my other-worldly experience. It was bright and colorful and drew a lot of attention. I hung it on the wall in the museum as well, with a short write-up of my visionary experience at the labyrinth.

All proceeds from the donations, sale of the books, room rental fees, items sold in the gift shop, and fees collected for yoga classes paid the utilities and other overhead expenses to keep the museum up and running. We donated 20 percent of the profit to Cherokee schools located on several Cherokee reservations nearby.

At the back door of the museum was a sign that said, *"This Way to the Labyrinth,"* with an arrow pointing outside where the trail that the spirits had formed with the flames began, leading to the labyrinth and the 5 villages.

David and Lori decided to rent the teepees in the villages to church groups, Boy Scouts, Girl Scouts, families, honeymooners, and others seeking a restful getaway or a walk in the labyrinth near the waterfall.

At least 3 times a week, I played the flute there in the center, 4 days if it was an extremely busy week. The museum also attracted lots of history seekers, and history teachers brought their classes on field trips and campouts.

The teepees were rented for $85 per night, and those proceeds kept the campsite open and paid for the cleaning and upkeep of the teepees and the village grounds. Beside the villages was an open space of land to play corn hole, basketball, croquette, and bad mitten, and visitors used it often. It brought many families together by creating quality fun, time, and memories.

We also used the open land for pow-wows and welcomed tribes from across the country to sell their goods and perform tribal dances. Of course, Cody also sold his artifacts and helped make Indian tacos during those events.

Beside the labyrinth were 2 benches where people could sit and relax, meditate, and enjoy the view. Jim placed one of the benches there in honor of his father. A silver-plated sign bolted to the top front of the bench read:

James Earl Hartwell, Sr.

1925–2018

"It's Me—It's Time"

I placed the other bench there in honor of the flute player. It said:

Cherokee Flute Player

Eternal Enlightener of the Soul

"We're Here—We're Here"

We all took turns volunteering our time to help at the museum. We made a monthly schedule and rotated duties among ourselves. Cleaning the building, making repairs, collecting donations, running the gift shop, ordering necessary supplies, etc. Cody and Connie mainly ran the gift shop.

We offered guided tours of the museum, labyrinth, and villages for groups of 5 or more for $25 each. Terry and I guided most of the tours; sometimes, Robin and Coy helped. Terry dressed up like the medicine man and Coy, the drummer. Robin and I dressed up in wrap-around deer skin skirts with Cherokee emblems on them and wore moccasins. The costumes sparked adventure and excitement among tourists. We also sold similar costumes at the gift shop.

Rob and Jeremy held ghost tours for $25 per person for those interested in the paranormal aspect of the land; they played their audio and video recordings on a wall-size screen with surround-sound speakers of the apparitions they'd seen and heard on camera and answered any questions that curiosity seekers had.

We all made ourselves available to greet guests at the museum or along the trail and at the labyrinth. We shared our own personal stories about hauntings we'd experienced and how the museum came to be, and we offered to answer their questions. It was a busy place, buzzing with the energy of enthusiastic sightseers and vacationers from nearly every state in the country. The museum was a success and helped put the small town of Sparta, Tennessee, on the map, so to speak.

Most out-of-towners who came discovered the surrounding beauty of the area and were intrigued by all the parks, the waterfall trails, kayaking adventures, hidden caves, small-town fairs, festivals, and all that nature has to offer here.

Jim came around every now and then when he felt like joining in the excitement but still battled bronchitis quite often, so he mostly stayed home. Lori informed us that his lungs were weak, and pneumonia had set in, so his recovery was taking a little longer than expected. We took turns taking his meals and doing some cleaning for him, and we picked up groceries when he needed us to.

Jessie mowed Jim's lawn as well as that of the museum grounds, and Donna planted pink, purple, and red tulips and gardenias to add color to the landscape. The land had regained its purpose and flourished with freshness and vitality. Everyone stayed busy with the common goal of honoring the original founders of the land and keeping alive their culture and traditions; the land was finally at peace again.

The museum had been open a year now, and no more evil paranormal activity had taken place there or anywhere on the land. No more diabolical and scary events. We hadn't seen the enlightened orbs either for a while, so I assumed they'd gone toward the light when they disappeared into the bonfire flames and were at peace in their reality as we were in ours.

Then, one evening in the labyrinth, just as I'd finished playing the flute, I saw it plain as day and thought my worst nightmare had revived itself. It was approaching nightfall, so all the guests had gone. A grey, smoky cloud hovered at the labyrinth entrance as though it was toying for my attention.

My heart sank. Not again, I mumbled audibly. What did it want? Why now, after all this time? Was it here to do harm and destroy everything we'd built? Would it transpose itself into a hideous creature like a shapeshifter or Tsau Ksui? We'd fought so hard to rid the land of evil. The thought of facing another fierce paranormal battle made me feel weary and fatigued.

I watched the smoke from afar as it glowered through the air and settled above Jim's rooftop. It must've hovered there for at least 5 minutes without moving, and then it turned pitch black and engulfed the whole house like a dense fog lingering after a humid storm.

I couldn't see the house at all, just a thick blob of fog hanging in the middle of nowhere. I watched it thin into a grey mist and vaporize into a bright light that sparkled through it like crystalline glass, then encompassed it with its brilliant rays. I sighed with relief, recognizing it as a sign from the enlightened orbs.

The light was bright white and as pure as the driven snow. It shined brighter and bolder. I couldn't look directly at it without blinking. I strained to keep my eyes open; I didn't want to miss it. It was beautiful, heavenly, angelic. I blinked a few times, then saw the sheeny essence rise upward toward the setting sun and disappear into its core. It left behind a pathway of gleaming rays that beamed to and from the sun to the house as though they were communicating in some psychical language that only their oneness understood.

I'm not sure how long the luminescence lingered there, but it was still there when I arrived home around 8:30. I was inspired and elated by the seraphic foreshadowing but also quite sad; *I knew what had happened.*

CHAPTER 18

I heard a knock at the front door. Terry answered it. I was in the back room folding laundry, and by the time I entered the living room, David and Lori were already sitting on the sofa. Their silence was as solemn as their faces and confirmed what I already knew. Terry and I sat down in the recliners across from them. We waited for them to speak first. I sat up straight in my chair and tried to be fully alert and prepared for the news.

"Uncle Jim passed away last night," said Lori, wiping away tears.

I never knew what to say during times like this, but my heart went out to them. I said the usual, "I'm so sorry, so very sorry." And I meant it.

I wanted to say more, but the mundane cliques that most people said during a time like this seemed so unhelpful and pointless. Things like, "He's in a better place." Or "At least he's no longer suffering." Or "He's always with us." Or "He didn't really leave; he's still here."

All those things that dampened a mood instead of uplifting it during a time like this.

"So sorry to hear that," said Terry. "It seemed like he was getting better; what happened?"

I hadn't told Terry about the luminescence yet; he was busy refurbishing his old '69 Firebird and worked in the garage until late, and I was asleep when he came to bed.

Lori tried to speak through tears and sobs but couldn't seem to choke out the words, so David took over.

"His pneumonia got worse," he said. "We took him to the ER 2 nights ago, and they gave him a shot and some antibiotics and kept him overnight. They sent him home the next day, and he was getting plenty of rest, drinkin' lots of fluids. His lungs were just too weak, I guess. We went over there last night to check on him about 8:15, and he passed away while we were there."

Silence fell among us. There was nothing to say or anything we could say that would dispel the sadness we all felt.

Finally, Lori said, "Do you mind lettin' the others know? That would take a load off if you could do that, and we'll keep you informed of any services or arrangements we make."

"Of course, anything," I said.

Then, I told them about the foreshadowing I'd seen walking home from the labyrinth yesterday evening. The gleaming light from the sun had shined down upon Jim's house while they were there during the time of his passing. It seemed to bring them comfort despite their sorrow.

As they left, we made them promise they'd call us if there was anything else we could do. They hugged us, thanked us, and promised to keep in touch as plans progressed.

I went to the museum to let the other team members know about Jim's death. Robin and Coy were there, and so were Connie and Cody. The news came as a shock to them, but as always, they wanted to pitch in and help. I called the other team members to tell them the news, and they were also ready to lend a hand. Everyone took turns preparing meals for the family and helping however they could. We closed the museum 2 days in his honor and hung a wreath on the front door saying, "RIP Jim Hartwell; you'll be missed."

We kept the labyrinth open, and most of us spent more time there contemplating his afterlife and saying prayers for him and the family members.

The family had Jim cremated and buried his ashes next to his wife Beverly's grave with a small headstone that had "Great Warrior" engraved on it. I'd never met Beverly, but Lori talked about "Aunt Beverly" often, and there was a picture of her and Jim hanging in Lori's hallway of Jim in that red flannel jacket and Beverly wearing a beautiful blue flowered dress.

Lori also had a bench placed alongside the labyrinth, beside Earl's, with a silver plate bolted to the top front that said:

James Earl Hartwell, Jr.

Founder of The White County Museum of the Cherokee

1945–2025

People came from miles around to attend Jim's Memorial Service, which was held outside at his gravesite. There must've been over 200 people who showed up to pay their last respects. Jim had lived in Sparta all his life, knew lots of people, and was well respected. Everyone who knew him was sad to hear of his passing and offered their condolences.

The celebration of his life was both glorious and somber. Among those who spoke were David, Lori, Coy, Terry, Cody, and Jessie, as well as several other relatives and personal friends of Jim's that I hadn't met before. They reminded the audience of fun times, moments of laughter, sorrow, and adventure as they recalled the memorable times with him throughout the years. Ginger sang *It is Well with My Soul* acapella and did a beautiful job. I played the flute as a benediction followed by a moment of silence.

After everyone left, I remained there with only the family members and played the flute for them as their last "Goodbye" meditation to Jim before moving on with the remainder of the day and their lives.

Playing the flute seemed to draw the presence of the flute player, and I saw him floating above Jim's grave site while I played for the family. After that day, I saw him often in the woods, at the labyrinth, and at the waterfall. I was glad he was back; his presence was comforting, and I welcomed it.

Sometimes, I'd find myself talking to him both telepathically and audibly, and he'd answer by putting thoughts in my head or feelings in the depth of my innermost being. Thoughts such as *Stay calm; there's a rough time ahead, but it will be okay.* Or, *Great warriors are strong and resilient, and you are one of those.*

186

He'd also whisper secrets of the tribe that brought the Unetlanvhi (Great Spirit) and guided me in which notes to play on my flute. I intuitively knew when he was around me, even when I couldn't see him. It was a bonded spirit connection that I couldn't explain but knew was real. It transcended all realities and had no time; it simply IS always.

About a month after Jim's passing, Connie and Cody announced their engagement and their desire to use the Gozho Room at the museum for their wedding ceremony and reception. After all, the group brought them together; it only seemed natural that they should share such a joyous occasion with the group.

Not long after, Rob and Ginger announced their wedding plans as well. After the two couples conversed, they decided to make it a double wedding and planned it for March 4 of the following year, which was the anniversary date of the grand opening of the museum.

Connie asked me to be her matron of honor since she and her only sister, Lindsey, had an estranged relationship. I gladly accepted and, of course, it gave me an opportunity to go shopping for a new dress. I chose a low-cut taupe dress made of silk. Arianna was Ginger's matron of honor and dressed in a stunning blue dress made of chiffon. All the guys served as ushers. Both brides' moms took charge of the reception, with Lori and Robin assisting. The weddings and the reception were small but joyous, with only a few family members and the team in attendance.

In the fall of that same year, Jessie and Donna announced their wedding plans, invited the whole team, and asked if they could reserve the Gozho Room as well. We all attended and hoped that Jessie's out-of-control mode was a thing of the past; it appeared that Donna had both tamed and warned him of the consequences.

The Gozho Room was used a lot for all kinds of occasions, and it helped bring families and friends together and caused the museum to prosper. The museum, the villages, and the labyrinth continued to be a great success, with at least 1,000 visitors per month. I stood in awe of the land, what we had accomplished here, and the enlightened spirits that had made it all possible.

Visitors in the labyrinth and in the villages reported seeing the enlightened orbs from time to time, as well as the flute player. They saw them in the woods, by the waterfall, at the labyrinth, out in the open field, and in the museum gardens. Wherever they appeared on the land, they brought light. Some heard the melodious flute tones during the night long after I'd finished playing mine at the labyrinth. I was glad these higher beings were there, protecting the land and bringing inspiration to all those who came.

Visitors also reported seeing an older gentleman dressed in blue jeans and a red flannel jacket who seemed to enjoy sitting on one of the benches in the labyrinth. I think it was the "Great Warrior." Beside him was a lady with golden brown hair, slightly graying, dressed in a blue flowered dress. They were often seen holding hands and conversing. It was obvious they were quite fond of each other.

Others saw him out and about every now and then on a riding lawnmower, which would appear and disappear in different places but mostly surrounding the museum.

Still, others caught a glimpse of him deep in the woods riding a 4-wheeler along some backwoods trails. I thought I saw him once at the end of the driveway, checking his mail.

On the bench beside them, an even older gentleman dressed in blue overalls and a blue cap sat there with his companion, a grey-haired lady dressed in a plain white cotton dress, which Lori confirmed was Sarah.

Their reunion appeared sweet and loving. Visitors also caught a glimpse of him in the museum, gliding above the Tsul Ksui statue, which we accepted as a sign that he was telling us that this was the creature he'd seen that triggered his death in the kitchen of the old house. A few other visitors reported seeing him appear to them, saying, "It's me, it's time."

Others reported seeing the 2 couples together engaging in what appeared to be a friendly and meaningful conversation. I'm sure they had a lot to get caught up on after all these years. I just smiled when I heard these reports. Several people captured pictures of these apparitions and sent them to me. I added them to a new and updated version of the *Haunted Journal*, which was underway and being edited day by day.

The evil and darkness that once inhabited the land were gone, and the land was filled with honor, respect, and tranquility. Visitors came and left feeling inspired, enlightened, and encouraged. It was a place of peace and rest. The kind of place they all came back to time and time again to rejuvenate and unwind from life's troubles.

I was proud to live here and proud to call the "team" my friends and neighbors. We couldn't have accomplished any of this without our team… and the *others*. I was glad they were here... *all* of them—glad that we were not alone and that *still there were others*.

About the Author

Vicki enjoys writing, painting, hiking, swimming, traveling, and being in the great outdoors in nature. She believes in honoring GOD and country above all. Also, she loves adventures, her family, and friends, and living her life in the mountains near lots of beautiful waterfalls. She is a small-town gal and a native Tennessean. At the same time, she is a mother, grandmother, and great-grandmother and is also a massage therapist and an experienced education instructor. Vicki lives with her husband, Terry, in Sparta, Tennessee.

Printed in Great Britain
by Amazon

36113184R00116